Mary Alford

Saving Agent Tanner
Covert Justice, Book 2

By
Mary Alford

ISBN-10:1-946939-05-6

ISBN-13:978-1-946939-05-0

Chapter One

Do you know what happened to Booth Tanner?

The text message was brief, chilling, and enough to send me back into the shadowy world I thought I'd left behind for good.

Booth Tanner. My husband and the man I once believed was my soul mate. Booth had been the love of my life. So much so that I still couldn't bring myself to sign the divorce papers after three years. He was the man whose name I hadn't spoken aloud in almost three years. I couldn't think of Booth and keep moving forward. I'd severed all ties with him. The life. The person I'd once been.

Which made the message infinitely more threatening in that someone had discovered our past connection.

I'd taken all the necessary precautions to keep my past secret from the diplomat I'd become today.

I glanced around the guest office I'd occupied for the

past three days of my visit to the States. Everything was as it had been since our team arrived on Monday, and yet...

My hands shook as I committed the phone number attached to the message to memory, somehow knowing it would be untraceable. After exhausting all of my former espionage skills, I came up empty handed. Whoever sent the chilling message wanted to remain anonymous.

I discreetly closed my door. Once I'd made sure my online identity and that associated with my computer couldn't be traced, I went to work. It took ten tries, eight more than it would have in the old days to crack the CIA's secure access code. Hidden in the usual jargon meant to confuse would-be hackers and those with more sinister motives in mind, were two words that jumped out at me.

Cowboy Sunset.

Booth's code name was Cowboy. He'd chosen it because he thought it was funny, being a huge Dallas Cowboy fan. Sunset was CIA speak for an agent gone missing.

Booth Tanner had gone missing.

It was a long time before I could breathe. Drawing air into my lungs became an impossible task.

It doesn't mean anything. Father, please don't let it mean anything.

What happened to Booth had nothing to do with me. He was no longer part of my heart or my life, I tried to convince myself.

I was still sitting there staring at those two words

trying to believe I'd put my relationship with Booth in the past when my second in command, Jeff Scott, walked into my office, unannounced. I hastily logged off the website, but not without raising Jeff's suspicions.

He stopped midway through the door and stared at me. He'd picked up the emotional firestorm the mere mention of Booth's name brought.

"You okay? You look as if you've seen a ghost or something. I'm not interrupting anything am I?"

He indicated the cell phone clutched in my hand and I struggled to regain some of my composure. "No, of course not. I'm fine." My glance fell on the text message. I didn't dare save the note. Best not to leave any connection to my past anywhere someone might readily check. I hit the delete button and the message disappeared.

I straightened a bit in my chair and squared my shoulders. "I guess it's being back in D.C. again. Come in, what's up?"

Jeff readily accepted my explanation. The excitement of our upcoming meeting with the Secretary of State prior to the start of the latest Israeli-Palestine peace talks had everyone from our embassy working overtime. The Secretary of State's impending visit to Jerusalem meant security would be at its highest. The entire team had been called back to the States to go over every possible threat before flying to Jerusalem at the end of the week.

News from my past could not have come at a worse possible time.

But this is Booth. He needs you.

"I'm finishing the final agenda plans for the SOS's arrival. We should be set for our meeting with her team at two."

I glanced at my watch, my mind working at breakneck speed. It was past ten D.C. time. I had four hours to find out what was happening in Booth's life that someone felt the need to bring me into his world again. And for what purpose?

"Great, look, Jeff, I have to step out for a little while. I'll be back before the meeting, of course," I assured him quickly when I spotted Jeff's initial shocked reaction.

"Are you sure you're okay?" His narrowed gaze bounced from the phone to hone in on my expression.

I reached back into my past, to the training I'd received by some of the best covert ops around and somehow managed to pull off indifference, then I grabbed the first excuse to come to mind. "Perfectly." I waved the phone in the air to emphasize the point. "An old friend. I promised I'd meet her for lunch today. She's having personal problems and needs a shoulder to cry on. I should be back by one at the latest."

Worry evaporated from Jeff's features and his carefree smile returned. "Oh, well, I can certainly understand. But if you're not back, don't worry. I can handle this one without you."

While there was a certain amount of genuine concern in his answer, the bottom line was Jeff wanted my job.

He'd been working under me for a year now and was tired of playing second fiddle to a woman. Jeff had the type of personality that thrived on challenge. He excelled in his work but had been growing bored for a while now.

As the assistant to the U.S. Ambassador to Israel, I was next in line for the ambassador's job when David Judah retired next year. Since Jeff had learned about David's upcoming retirement, he'd been angling for a closer relationship with him. Jeff knew how much David valued punctuality and teamwork. No excuse would be good enough for his second in command being a no-show for a meeting. In spite of the fact that the meeting was simply to go over the schedule with the SOS's team. David would be there. He'd expect his team there as well. That went double for me.

"That's okay. As I said, I'll be back in plenty of time." I grabbed my cell phone and tucked it into the pocket of my jacket, then almost as an afterthought undocked the laptop and took it with me. I had no reason to believe Jeff would sink low enough as to go through my computer documents, but then I had hacked into confidential CIA files. It was best not to take any unnecessary risks.

I left diplomatic headquarters located in the shadow of the Capitol building, ignoring the string of cabs sitting out front. No need to draw undue attention to myself. Besides, I could walk the five-plus blocks quicker than a cabbie would maneuver his way through the congested morning traffic.

While I walked at a fast click, I called Dana McIntyre's phone. Dana was my daughter Ava's nanny. I'd first met her a year earlier while assigned to the embassy in Israel. Dana was a theology student who'd recently graduated from Trinity Bible School and was taking a sabbatical from her studies to pursue another lifelong dream.

Dana wanted to see the Holy Land. She'd jumped at the chance to live in Jerusalem and had fallen in love with Ava right from the start. But for me, well, old habits die hard. I'd done an extensive background check on Dana who proved to be the real deal and a blessing.

"Hi there, Rach, what's up?" I could hear my daughter's excited gibbering in the background.

Although I was worried, Ava's sweet voice had a way of grounding me and reminding me I wasn't part of that life anymore. I was being paranoid. "How is she? What are you two up to this morning?"

"She's terrific, aren't you, pumpkin. We're finishing up breakfast. Someone wanted to sleep in today."

"Is she feeling okay?" My daughter never slept past seven.

"Yes, she's fine, *Mommy*. Suffering from jet lag I suppose. Don't worry."

As if. "Listen, Dana, I know you two were going to the park today, but do me a favor and stay home. Keep her inside or if you go out, play in the backyard."

"Anything wrong?" Dana picked up on my worry. I was definitely losing my touch.

I forced myself to relax. "No, at least…I'm not sure. To be safe, don't leave the property today, okay?"

After a moment's hesitation, she agreed. "Sure. No problem."

"Oh and if anyone comes around you don't recognize, don't answer the door and if you see anyone hanging around the place call me immediately."

Another tick in time slipped by. "Will do." I could hear the questions in her voice. Dana knew everything about my past. I'd been honest with her from the beginning. She knew I wasn't just being a worried mom.

With that small amount of reassurance, I could breathe again. "I'll explain everything tonight. In the meantime, keep your eyes open."

While it had been years since I'd left D.C. behind, it seemed nothing had changed. At exactly eleven a.m., I spotted the person I was looking for. His car had been easy to pick out. I simply searched for the flashiest, most expensive one I could find in the parking garage and waited for its owner to emerge.

Agent Michael Bernard didn't disappoint. I waited until he'd unlocked the Porsche before materializing from behind the concrete support beam next to the passenger door.

"Is it true?"

Agent Bernard did a double take. The fact that I'd taken him by surprise easily spoke volumes as to why Michael was for the most part an administrative person and not a field agent.

"Rachel, what are you doing here?"

He seemed genuinely surprised to see me, which answered one question. Michael was not the one who texted me.

I slammed my palms against the top of the Porsche. "Is it true?"

He didn't pretend not to know what I was talking about. Michael simply got into the car and waited for me to do the same.

Once I'd slid into the low-slung car, he turned the key and the car's powerful engine roared to life. Michael cranked the stereo to full volume and left the parking garage. He drove half a block away then pulled into the parking lot of a strip mall.

"How did you find out?"

Michael's stall for time confirmed my answer.

"Is Booth missing?"

He lowered the volume a decimal then turned in his seat to watch me carefully. "Why do you care? You wrote him out of your life three years ago."

Those words still hurt to hear. They weren't true of course, but that's what Booth believed and what I'd let Michael think as well.

"Someone sent me a text message this morning. Someone knows about Booth and my past. If they know about my connection, they'll know about Ava. So, I need to know. Is it true?"

"Who texted you?" His habit of answering a question with another was infuriating at the best of times. Today, I was not in the mood to play games. I hated being drawn back into the shadow games, a slang term used by agents across the board to describe the shadow war they fought behind the scenes which most Americans were not aware of.

"I don't know," I managed through gritted teeth. I watched him carefully as I added, "I thought maybe it was you."

"Yeah, right. You're the last person I'd want involved in this."

Michael's contempt was clear. It was hard to believe

we'd once been friends. "Then answer the question."

His next words ripped away what small amount of hope I'd been clinging to since receiving the text. "Rachel, he's..."

"Sunset. I know. Where?"

"Rachel, you know I can't tell you anything more. Let it go. It's not your problem anymore. Stay out of it, okay?"

I closed my eyes, wishing I could do as he asked. "Where. Where did he go missing? Michael, tell me."

"Near Kandahar."

"Oh no." This was everyone in the spy business's worst nightmare come to fruition. How could this happen to someone as highly skilled as Booth?

Speaking the next question aloud took everything inside of me. "Is he alive?"

Michael blew out a deep breath. "Does it matter? Why do you care? This has nothing to do with you anymore, Rachel. You wanted out. You're out. Let it be. We'll handle it. Go back to your pretty little diplomatic lifestyle and leave the real patriotism to those who have the stomach for it."

I ignored Michael's familiar jab. "What are you going to do?" His silence confirmed the seriousness of Booth's position. "You can't leave him there. Michael, he's your friend."

He shifted in his seat to glare at me. "He's behind enemy lines. We haven't heard from him in days. If he isn't dead, he's been captured. Either way, we can't help him. Booth can take care of himself. If he's physically able, he'll find a safe house and contact us."

"If? Michael, you can't leave him there."

He turned away. His stony expression made it clear he hated my involvement. "It's out of my hands." He continued to stare straight ahead, not looking at me. I knew what that meant. Booth had been sent on an "unscheduled" mission.

Which meant no one but Booth's handler knew where he was. Wherever he'd been sent, he'd gone there to kill someone big.

I leaned into Michael's line of sight, forcing him to look at me. "That's ridiculous and you know it." When he didn't answer, I reached for the door handle and made to leave the car. "Fine, but I won't stand by and let him die because your people sent him out as a ghost."

I yanked the handle and tried to open it, but Michael grabbed my hand. "Stay out of this, Rachel. You don't know what's involved here. I'm warning you, if you get in the way, I'll personally have you arrested."

The steely resolve in my voice surprised me. I knew he could carry out that promise and more, but Michael wasn't the only one with a few cards left to play. "Try it and I'll forget I owe you anything and go public with what I know. I think there are a few things Hughes and your precious CIA wouldn't want Joe Blow Public knowing."

Michael took the threat as real. We both knew I had enough details to bring certain key people in the CIA to their knees.

"You wouldn't dare. Rachel, you owe me your life and your child's. If it weren't for me, you'd probably be dead by now."

"Maybe, but I owe Booth something more."

The sneer in his otherwise handsome features told me he didn't believe my motives. "I'd say it's a little late for that, don't you think? You didn't think twice about dropping Booth from your life the minute he was no longer convenient for you. You never bothered telling him he's a father."

I jerked away from Michael's restraint and shoved the door open. "I'm not having this discussion with you again. If you won't help Booth, then I will." I got out of the car then turned back and leaned into the open door. "And if you don't have enough nerve to stand up to your commander and help your best friend fight for his life then stay out of my way."

Chapter Two

Brave words. I'd barely made two blocks before I'd begun to regret voicing my intentions to Michael. He'd probably been on the phone to his superior officer before I cleared the first block.

The information I had to work with was next to none. I didn't know where Booth might have gone missing beyond somewhere near Kandahar. In that particular region of Afghanistan, there were virtually miles and miles of rugged terrain, mountainous caves reputed to have hidden the worst terrorist known in U.S. history. Booth could be hiding anywhere amongst the caves. He could be held captive. He could be dead.

I slowed my steps as I tried to formulate a plan. With my diplomatic position, I could find a way to travel to the area without drawing too much attention to myself. But if the wrong people were to find out that I was of Jewish heritage, not to mention my former history with the CIA, then I might find myself in the same position as Booth.

I couldn't think about Booth or the history we shared and not worry about my daughter.

Michael had been right about one thing, though. I owed him an awful lot. My life. Ava's. Thanks to Michael, I'd been lucky enough to get out. Booth couldn't, or more to the point, wouldn't leave the CIA. He lived for the thrill of the game we played, and in the beginning, I'd been attracted to the adrenaline rush as well. Booth's drive and determination, his dangerous edge, had been an incredibly handsome before we became...involved. Afterward, well, the tension and constant fear we faced well, it just made him that much more attraction.

Unfortunately, it didn't take long before living in the shadow of death, the constant fear of being found out by the enemy, took its toll on me and my marriage with Booth.

The thrill began to pale in comparison to the risk. But it was the realization that no matter how many enemy threats we stopped, there would be thousands of new recruits waiting in the wings as determined to complete their mission that had finally done it for me. I'd fell back on my faith in God after leaving Booth and the CIA. If I hadn't had that faith, I think I would have lost it.

I'd seen things with Booth I wished I could purge from my memory. Horrible things that brought home the reality of how truly evil human beings could be. Especially when they believed in a cause. Terrorism was a name attached to a belief, depending on which side you were on, either terrorist or patriot. I'd come to realize, when threatened enough, the most civilized person could become a terrorist.

Some within the same agencies sworn to have our country's best interest at heart.

* * * *

"She knows." Michael watched as Rachel Weiss disappeared around the corner of Washington and James. It only took a second for the impact of his statement to hit home.

"How did this happen?" Director Tom Hughes demanded in the loud thunderous voice he'd become famous for when properly angered.

For reasons Michael couldn't begin to explain, he decided to keep details of his conversation with Rachel between them. He'd do a little checking on his own. She was right about one thing. He owed as much to Booth.

"Don't know."

"She's a problem. She knows too much. We need to have someone keep an eye on her."

Michael could almost read Hughes' mind. "Don't worry," he said. "I'll take care of it."

"You'd better," The director added with the implication clear. "I don't want her coming back to bite us. This thing is too important."

Michael hit the end call button without answering.

"Booth. Why'd you have to go and get yourself in trouble?" He couldn't think about the possibility Booth might be dead. Booth had always seemed invincible, like Superman. Had Superman finally met his kryptonite?

He'd been friends with Booth since their college years at V-Tech. He was closer to Booth than he was with his own brothers, which was why he'd cautioned Booth about getting involved with Rachel from the beginning. Mostly because he'd never seen him react the way he had to Rachel with any other woman. For her, he'd almost been willing to give it all up. Would have, too, if it hadn't been for Michael.

There was no way Michael was going to let his friend throw it all away for a woman.

Now, Michael glanced around the parking lot, examining the most innocent of activities with the experience of someone trained to spot a covert threat. A habit he couldn't shake. Booth's disappearance had him spooked.

It had everyone at the Agency spooked, including Director Hughes.

Michael fired the car's engine, not bothering with lowering the volume of the state-of-the-art sound system. Someone needed to be tracking Rachel Weiss' movements right away.

"Yello, Sam here." Sam Masters, Michael's subordinate, might be still wet behind the ears, but he had all the makings of becoming one of the great ones, like Booth. Michael could see the same self-assuredness Booth possessed at that age. It would take Sam far in the business if he didn't let his emotions get in the way as Booth had.

"I need you and Henry to tail someone and keep me

updated."

"Okay. Will do. Shoot. What's the name and where can we find him?"

"Her. It's a her. Rachel Weiss."

Sam blew out a long slow whistle. "The Assistant Ambassador to Israel? Is someone threatening her or does this have something to do with the ambassador himself?"

"Neither. At least not as far as I'm aware of. Keep an eye on her and I need you to have someone watch her house. She and her young daughter are staying at Houston Avenue along with the nanny."

"Someone's done his homework. Got it. We'll take care of it."

Michael ignored the typical Sam smart aleck comment. Since Rachel left the CIA, he'd made a promise to Booth and himself to keep an eye out for her. Michael had made it a point of keeping both Rachel and her daughter under his protective care. He'd known she was back in the States, but when Booth went missing things got hairy. He hadn't expected her to find out, much less care about what happened to Booth anymore.

"Oh and Sam, she doesn't know I've asked you to do this. Make sure it stays that way."

He was ready to end the call when he remembered the text message Rachel mentioned that started this whole thing in motion. "And I need you to pull Rachel's cell phone records. I want to know who's been calling her since she arrived here and in the days prior to leaving Jerusalem."

"Got it. I'll let you know the minute I have

anything."

* * * *

"Ah, Rachel, there you are. Is everything okay with Ava? Jeff told me you had to take care of some personal business." Ambassador Judah, always an affectionate man, engulfed me in one of his world-renowned bear hugs. I'd arrived outside the Secretary of State's offices with minutes to spare, hot and exhausted from the long walk.

When I could breathe calmly enough to speak, I tried to keep from showing the man I'd come to love as a father all of my fears. "Oh, no. No, Ava's fine. I was talking with a friend having some marital troubles." I tossed Jeff a stern look. This underhanded get-ahead-at-all-costs thing was starting to wear thin. Once I took over the helm of ambassador in a few months, I'd have a serious talk with Jeff about his future.

"Good, good. I don't want anything bad happening to my goddaughter." I smiled at Jeff's surprise. He knew I was close with David, but he had no idea David and his wife Hannah were Ava's godparents.

"Jeff tells me we're all set for our meeting with the secretary's team." In the almost three years I'd worked with David, I don't think I'd ever caught him in a bad mood. At sixty-eight, he'd served his country with an honor and grace that made me proud to be both an American.

"Yes, we have every minute of her visit to Jerusalem prepared. I think her team will be pleased."

"I'm sure of it. I trust your judgment implicitly, Rachel. But let's not keep them waiting. I adore Madam Secretary, but that Martin scares me."

* * * *

"Gentleman and lady." David spared me an affectionate grin. "I believe we are all in agreement. Given that all the added security procedures go into place without any unforeseen issues, the peace talks will begin on the twentieth. The Secretary of State will arrive two days prior to allow for any additional preparation."

The SOS's team of five men nodded in agreement.

"Excellent. Then we'll see each of you in two weeks. Have a pleasant journey to the Holy Land."

David waited until the car was on its way before assessing the outcome of the meeting. "I believe that went well. Rachel and Jeff, I thank you both for your diligence."

I smiled, hoping David couldn't sense my distraction.

"I couldn't agree more." Jeff seemed thrilled by the vote of confidence.

The limo came to a seamless halt in front of our makeshift offices. "I'll drop the two of you off. Hannah and I have dinner plans with friends for the evening. I'll see each of you on the plane tomorrow."

My hesitation further peaked David's curiosity. "David, do you think I could have a moment of your time?" I saw Jeff glance my way and added, "It's a personal matter."

"Of course, of course. Ride with me. I can have the car drop you off at your quarters."

"Thank you, David."

We said our goodbyes to Jeff and made our way through the light early afternoon D.C. traffic in silence for a while. I didn't know how to ask for David's help. He knew most of my secrets. I'd long ago explained my past life to David. After all, it would come up in the background check.

The compassion and gentle concern he and Hannah showed me while I mended my broken heart and made my way through pregnancy and single parenthood had been a gift from God.

Next to me, his soft chuckle intruded into my troubled thoughts. "Will you have me guess what's troubling you, child?"

I turned to him. I'd almost forgotten how intense those gray eyes could be. As if he was searching my soul.

It was part of his magic. David had the personality of a kindly grandfather and the sharp intellect of a wise teacher. It had served him well throughout his career. David could relate to anyone.

I smiled at him. "No. I'm sorry. This is hard. David, it's Booth. He's gone missing," I added reluctantly as if admitting this truth to someone else was like accepting my fate.

When I first took the job as assistant ambassador, I'd stayed with David and Hannah. They'd witnessed more than I wished they had during that time. It had been all my decision to leave Booth, but that hadn't made it any easier, getting over him or moving forward with my life without him in it.

David was silent for a moment. Another stalwart piece of his character. He considered all options before weighing in on a problem.

"I see. Do you have any idea where?"

"Yes. Near Kandahar."

"Dangerous ground, Rachel. Especially for a Jew." He eyed me carefully. "What do you need to do?" He phrased it as a question, but he knew.

"I have to go there."

"You think that's wise, my dear? I know he's Ava's father and you still have feelings for him, but you're not part of that world anymore. Perhaps it's best to leave this matter to those still in the game."

It was hard telling the truth. "I can't. They aren't planning on doing anything to help him."

This would be hard for him to fathom. David saw only the good in people. In spite of the work we did, he chose to believe most people possessed goodness in them. On those few times when the dark side of human nature crept into his world and I tried to get him to see the truth, David would stubbornly refuse.

"He's one of their own. They can't leave him behind."

If only that were true. "They can and they will. David, Booth's mission wouldn't necessarily have been sanctioned by the powers that be. He was going after someone big. His orders would be to kill. If it's an unsanctioned hit, they can't send anyone to help him."

David made no bones about his distaste for the

tactics used by some of our intelligence departments in the war on terror.

"I see. And if you go there, what will you do? What do you hope to accomplish?"

"I still have some contacts around. I'll try to ask a few questions, see what I can learn on my own."

"You know you have my support no matter what you choose to do, but you understand that I cannot bring the embassy in on this."

"Of course." The implications could be enormous, especially with the upcoming peace talks between Israel and Palestine. If any hint of someone from our team working covert ops behind enemy lines were to reach the ears of the Palestine government, the small amount of progress we'd made so far would come crashing down around us.

"I know. I'll be okay, don't worry."

"But I do worry about you going back into that world again, Rachel, I cannot lie. I remember how hard it was for you to leave it in the past. What happens if you learn that Booth has been captured or worse, dead?"

My reaction must have shown on my face. "I don't know. But I have to try to find out the truth for Ava's sake."

"For Ava or for yours?" he asked gently.

I shook my head. "For both of us, I guess. David, I owe Booth."

He didn't agree, but after another moment, he let it go. "All right. What can I do to help you? I can pave the way. Get you there, but you must know Rachel, there are places there that are like going back into time a thousand years. Women are still considered property. A Jewish woman alone could be in grave danger. *Your* life could be in danger. What would happen to Ava's future if something were to happen to you? She needs you."

"I'm not going to risk my life. I know what I'm doing. But I'd like for Dana and Ava to stay with you and Hannah while I'm gone."

"Of course, but will you let me send some people with you? I'd feel better."

"No, I can't let you do that. It would be disastrous if my involvement were traced to you in any way. Besides, I'll call less attention to myself and have better luck traveling alone."

David had known this was what my answer would be. "I understand. How long do you need?"

"I won't be sure until I know more about what I'm up against. I hope to have something within a few days. I'll leave as soon as we return to Jerusalem and I know that Ava is settled in with you."

"I see. Well, you have no worries about Ava. Absolutely we will watch over your baby girl for you."

"There's one more thing. If anything happens to me, promise me you'll take care of her."

"Rachel..."

"David, please promise me. I need you to do this for me."

He patted my hand affectionately. "You know that we will. You come home safely."

"I'll do my best. And David, if Booth should survive and I don't. Don't tell him about her. Don't tell him he has a daughter."

With another graze nod, David was deposited at his home outside of the city, and the driver took me to the brownstone I'd borrowed for our stay from an old pre-CIA acquaintance.

My thoughts spun as the driver pulled in front of the two-story building. Parked a few yards down the street, we'd passed a black, nondescript sedan. Instinctively, I knew Michael was having me watched. I'd need to be careful, follow as closely as possible to my normal routine in order not to draw any unnecessary attention. If they were watching me here, there'd be no doubt in my mind they'd be scrutinizing my every move once I'd returned to Jerusalem.

I'd made a mistake by going to Michael. I should have realized the seriousness of Booth's position.

"I'm home," I called out to Dana once I'd unlocked the door.

"We're in here." I followed Dana's voice into the kitchen where I found her and Ava making cookies. My daughter had been waiting for me to come in. She held up two cookies and grinned her wide, toothy grin. All of my fears melted away as I knelt and held open my arms.

Ava barreled toward me with all the enthusiasm of a two-year-old who hadn't seen her mommy in hours. I scooped her up and lavished her with hugs and kisses until she was giggling uncontrollably and could barely contain herself.

She all but shoved one of the chocolate chip cookies in my mouth. "Mmm. Delicious," I said through bites.

Her tiny arms wrapped around my neck, her face inches from mine. I could feel cookie crumbs sprinkling down and inside my shirt.

"What have you and Dana been up to today, my dumpling?"

Using her pet name always made her giggle.

"We fed squirrels in the backyard and then we made cookies," Dana told me.

I mouthed a quick thank you over Ava's golden head. "That's nice. Did you two pack?"

Ava eagerly nodded. "Yes, Mommy."

I saw Dana cringe and somehow managed to suppress my own laughter.

"Good girl. Why don't we grab some milk and enjoy these cookies? Come on, Dana, you too."

Dana grabbed three glasses while Ava, still in my arms, pulled out the milk from the fridge. We sat at the kitchen table and devoured almost all of the cookies and I was careful not to show my baby any of my worries.

"Okay, you, bath time," I told her when I glanced at my watch and caught the time.

"Aw, Mommy. I want to help Dana with dinner."

"You can help her set the table. Come on."

Once dinner was over and Ava was in bed, I motioned Dana into the living room, turned on the TV as loudly as I dared and told Dana what was happening.

Once I'd finished with the sketchy details of Booth's fate, I added, "I'll need you and Ava to stay with the ambassador for a while. A few days."

"Oh, Rachel, do you think that's wise? Afghanistan is such a dangerous place."

"I know, but I have to do this."

Dana understood all the reasons why I couldn't leave

Booth behind. Slowly, she let go of her protests and said, "Okay. I'll say a prayer that God will keep you safe."

Chapter Three

For a city that was at the root of two religions' constant dispute, Jerusalem was both crowded and a little dirty.

The embassy's jet touched down on the Israeli national airbase. Within minutes, we were on our way to our perspective houses. During the flight, I'd explained briefly to Ava that I needed to go away for a few days. While she was upset to be separated from me, she loved spending time at David and Hannah's home because they had a dog that had had puppies. I promised her when I got back she could take one of those puppies home with her.

I left David with an assurance that I'd accept his offer for transportation into Afghanistan. He'd arranged for an Afghani friend of his to get me safely across the border. I'd told him I'd be operating under an alias so his friend wouldn't be expecting to escort a Rachel Weiss across the border.

Because I didn't trust that my phone or anyone else's close to me might not be bugged, David used the secured line on the plane reserved for embassy use only to call his contact. His friend agreed to our meeting place and told him he could get me as far as Kabul. After that, I'd be on my own.

With our luggage stowed away, we drove straight to David's house. Once I'd made sure Ava and Dana were safely settled in, I went back to my house in the city. It wasn't unusual for Ava to spend time with David. I hoped anyone watching us had done their research.

In the basement of our little home, on the top shelf of a metal bookcase, I'd hidden away a box filled with pieces of my past. The only thing I'd saved from that time.

I dragged the box upstairs then did a quick sweep of the house. As I expected, the phones were bugged. While the ambassador's residence wasn't being watched, mine was a different story. I spotted my shadow parked some distance away yet close enough to see whoever came and went from the house.

"Perfect," I said with an exasperated sigh. I'd have to be careful tomorrow.

Inside the box, I found my Glock. Its cold steel barrel reminded me of the last time I'd used it. It was still so fresh and raw that it could have been yesterday.

Booth and I'd been in Basra. I'd found out I was pregnant. I'd been scared to death of losing my child and arguing with myself over telling Booth about the baby.

We'd been tracking a lead on one of Bin Laden's generals. We'd spent the night hidden away in a remote cave. And as usual, we'd argued. I think Booth knew we were finished. After all the anger, resentment, and pain I'd gone through after our breakup, I couldn't push that memory from my heart. That had been the night Booth made it clear where I stood in his heart, and it would never be first.

"Rachel, you know I love you, but this is what I do. It's more than that, it's who I am. I can't shut it off. I thought it was who you were as well. The work we're doing is important. It could be the difference between freedom and extinction for the next generation." I hadn't been able to tell him the next generation was our child. And I couldn't risk our child's life any longer.

I knew if I lived long enough to get out of the country alive, I'd have to end it with him.

That had been the hardest decision I'd ever made. Letting go of Booth. Long after Booth left me to stand watch that night, I'd cried myself to sleep with the realization that I would always take second place in his heart.

In the days and weeks that followed, though there were times when I'd wake up in the middle of the night and could almost feel him next to me, I knew I'd made the right decision in leaving the CIA and Booth. Our relationship had been combustible from the first moment.

Booth was the one who'd recruited me. At the time, I was determined to go to Quantico. Booth convinced me I'd waste my talents at the FBI. I could do much more for my country hands-on.

Booth made falling in love with him so easy. He

took risks no normal human being could survive. For Booth, living on the edge, risking his life every second of the day was what made him tick.

I gave myself a mental shake. With a whole lot of difficulty, I let go of those memories.

Along with the Glock, I'd kept all of my old fake IDs. I found one that came close to my current look then shoved the rest inside a hidden compartment of my purse along with the Glock and the prepaid phone I'd purchased. I prayed I wouldn't have to use any of the pieces from my past, especially my training.

With my weapon secured, I packed only a few essentials along with a change of clothing into my laptop bag.

Adrenaline pumped through my body like fire, making sleep impossible. Whether I liked it or not, I was back in the game.

I'd be picked up by the car service the embassy used early the following morning, as was my normal routine. From there, David's friend would meet me four blocks away at the old market and take me into dangerous grounds. The part of Afghanistan where Booth reportedly went missing was a known Taliban stronghold.

When another hour passed and I still couldn't sleep, I pulled out my laptop and tried to get into the CIA database once more. It took longer than usual to crack the code this time. I'd given away too much to Michael by mentioning the code word sunset. He would have alerted the security team to a possible threat.

Once I'd broken the security code, I had only a few

minutes.

After I'd read past the jargon, the best I could conclude was that his handler heard from Booth for the last time some two days before his radio signal disappeared.

The last location of the signal had been at the foothills of the Aldean Mountains.

Booth had officially been missing almost a week without any contact. The chances of finding an operative alive after three days was about ten percent.

"Where are you, Booth? Why couldn't you let someone else handle this one for once?"

I could almost hear him laughing and chiding me. *"Let someone else take charge? Feel the rush? Experience the glory? Never."*

I glanced at the clock. After two, Jerusalem time. I shut down the computer without any answers. I needed to try and sleep. While the drive to Kabul wouldn't be long, it would be hard. I'd need to prepare for the most difficult mission I'd ever have to face. Bringing Booth home. Dead or alive.

* * * *

"Do I know you?" I'd noticed him right away. I was barely two steps from my apartment when I spotted him following me. At first, I'd had the crazy thought that perhaps this was some new test the FBI had put into place. Were they trying to see if their new recruits had what it took?

I turned the corner and waited for him to catch up

with me. *He hadn't been surprised by the move or the least bit daunted.*

"No, but I am about to save your life." Booth's cockiness was part of his charm. Shaggy blond hair touched his collar. He pushed it from his face with a carefree hand.

He wasn't the type of man who spent time worrying about his looks. He didn't need to. There was always a swarm of women attracted to Booth Tanner. The warmth in his smile crinkled the corners of his eyes. His hazel eyes danced with mischief.

His strange answer made me wonder if perhaps he was playing for the wrong side. Naively, I asked the question he'd hoped. "What are you talking about?"

"I'm going to save your life. I'd hate to see anyone as talented as you, Rachel Weiss, waste their talents on such boring stuff as you'll be doing at the Bureau."

That he knew my name threw me, which amused Booth. "How did you...?"

"Trust me. I know more about you than you do about yourself."

I decided he must be some crackpot. I turned and started to walk away. "I've heard enough. Goodbye."

He caught up with me easily enough. His lean six-foot frame swallowed up my much shorter stride. "I'm Booth Tanner, by the way. I'm here to offer you a job with the CIA."

His out of the blue offer stopped me dead in my tracks. "The CIA? What are you talking about? Who are you?"

He took my question as consent to take my hand and

lead me to a quiet little coffee shop ironically in the shadow of the Hoover Building.

I waited until he'd ordered two coffees and we were seated in a corner booth away from curious onlookers. "I'm sorry, but I'm late. I have an appointment in less than two minutes."

As I was soon to learn, Booth was the type of person who did things at his own pace. "I know. As I said, I know everything about you. You'll go through their training in about a year and you'll be assigned to a desk for another. Then, if you're lucky, you'll get out in the field. I'm promising you with your talents and my influence and training, you'll be seeing field duty in six months. Tops. You'll be making a difference with us, Rachel. With the Bureau, you'll be another grunt."

That I'd stayed and listened to his whole spiel was a miracle in itself. Booth's offer was about as unorthodox as it got for me. Until I met him, my most daring maneuver had been applying to the FBI's Behavioral Science Division.

By the time we left the coffeehouse some two hours later, I was all crazy about Booth. By the following afternoon, I'd become gainfully employed. I was a member of an elite group within the CIA and Booth took more than a professional interest in me. And I was well on my way to falling in love with Booth Tanner.

* * * *

The alarm clock shrilled into the stillness of the predawn hours, dispelling troubled dreams of Booth. It felt as if I'd barely fallen asleep, but hours had passed and I was crying.

I hadn't cried for Booth in a long time. But this dream had been different. I'd relived the first time I met Booth. I could almost feel that little electric spark I experienced the first time he kissed me. The first moment I knew I loved him.

I showered and dressed in my most comfortable work attire. By the time the car arrived, I was somewhat more prepared for what lay ahead of me.

The driver buzzed the door. I opened it and smiled. "Hello, Luis."

Always formal, Luis never broke from protocol, which meant he was polite at all times but kept his distance by not forming any personal connections with those he serviced.

"Good morning, Ms. Weiss."

Luis opened the door for me and silently waited. Once we were on our way through deserted streets, I glanced behind us. A car pulled out a few yards away. Luis caught it as well.

"Is there a problem, ma'am?"

I hoped my smile was reassuring enough. The car service that the embassy employed was no normal limo business. The drivers were trained by the Mossad, the Israeli Intelligence Agency. "No, Luis, everything is fine." Another tense moment passed while I held my breath and Luis assessed the car tailing us. He'd obey my wishes to a certain point.

We arrived at the embassy an hour earlier than my scheduled time. When Luis questioned this, I told him I needed to catch up on paperwork. I stalled in the car, fiddling with my papers while keeping a close eye on the car behind us. It slid into a parking space some fifty yards back.

I glanced at my watch. I had fifteen minutes to get through the embassy's state of the art security and get out of the building to my meeting place.

"Thanks, Luis. See you tonight." I waved and began the first of several grueling security procedures.

Once I'd cleared the last checkpoint, I forced myself to walk casually to the elevator. There would be no way of knowing who might be watching me. I unlocked my office, did a quick check for anything out of the norm, then hurried from the building by the back security entrance reserved for emergencies only.

I ran the four blocks to where a nondescript gray Jeep waited for me in record time. The driver got out the second he spotted me.

"I was getting ready to leave without you. Miss Ingalls, I believe?"

"Yes, and I'm sorry. I was...held up."

He studied me carefully. "You'll understand when I tell you I need to see your ID."

"Of course." I pulled out the old ID for Laura Ingalls and waited while he studied the photo and then me. He didn't buy the name on my ID, but he'd gotten all the proof he needed.

"Nice job on the ID. Only a pro would know the truth." He handed it back to me and extended his hand. "Anwar Sayyid."

"Thank you." I didn't bother with any further

explanation and he wasn't expecting one. I had no idea how David knew someone who obviously was not on the up and up, but in this instance, I was grateful he did.

"Get in." Anwar didn't wait for an answer. He headed back to the driver side and I slipped into the seat opposite his clutching my laptop bag against my chest.

"How long before we arrive at the border?"

He tossed me a look as if to say, *foolish American.* "Eighteen hours if we drive straight through. You should get some sleep. You'll need to be sharp to get across that border."

I settled into the uncomfortable seat and let myself consider the risks I'd be taking along with the danger I'd face. I hadn't spoken to Booth since the night I told him it was over between us. I would probably be the last person on earth he'd want to see again and yet no one from his precious CIA was coming to save him. Whether he wanted my help or not, he was getting it.

* * * *

"Rachel, I care about you, but I can't offer you the fairy tale. It's not in me. I'm not the white picket fence kind of guy." His calloused hands framed my face. "I want you. More than I've ever wanted another woman. And if marriage is what you need to be comfortable with us, then let's get married." Booth smiled his smile that always got to me and yet his heartbreaking words pierced through my heart. I'd thought. I wanted...so much more.

He kissed me long and hard and the usual breathless

feeling made my knees weak. Why did he have to kiss like that? Look so good. Why did I have to fall for...Booth?

"It has to be your choice. Whatever you decide, I'll abide by your decision. You know where to find me," he said with another earth-shattering kiss and then he left me and I spent the rest of the evening arguing with my heart. I loved him. He wanted me. There would be nothing but heartbreak in my future, but it didn't matter. I loved him and I needed him like I needed my next breath. There would be plenty of time for regrets in the future and they would come. Tonight, well, the team would be leaving for Afghanistan the following morning. Who knew what the future held. I worry about my broken heart when and if I returned.

I couldn't bear to be alone any longer. I grabbed my keys and headed out to be with him.

I stood outside his house for a long time, right and wrong doing their usual battle. Then I rang the doorbell half hoping he wouldn't be home.

That night, we woke a Justice of the Peace and had a rushed wedding, so unlike all the beautiful weddings I'd dreamed of as a little girl. But that night, I didn't care. I was with Booth and that was all that mattered.

Someone nudged my arm. "We'll be arriving in fifteen minutes."

I roused myself from the bittersweet memory. I'd been staring out the window remembering the time when he'd told me where we stood with each other. Reliving those moments left me shaking from raw emotion. I could almost feel the heartache I'd experienced that night. Taste his lips against mine. I shook off the remnants of the dream with difficulty.

"Thank you, Anwar," I said and my voice sounded husky with emotion. If Anwar noticed the difference in me, he kept it to himself and I forced myself to get a grip. I'd need my wits about me to survive this thing and hopefully find Booth. For Ava's sake, I told myself. I was doing this for my daughter alone.

The sight that unfolded before me was like nothing I'd expected. I'd been to Kabul a handful of times in the past, all with Booth. Kabul had been one of the first cities liberated by the joint forces following the attacks of 9/11. Back then, it was still easy to tell the difference between good and evil because the lines hadn't yet been blurred in the name of justice.

We'd all been humbled by the gratitude the citizens of Kabul had shown their liberators. The excitement was easy to catch. The streets crowded with people who couldn't believe they were no longer under the Taliban's thumb.

Liberating Kabul had been romantic. Booth and I had spent our honeymoon in a house that had been abandoned by Taliban. With the city free of threats, there was a period of peace. We'd taken advantage of those days, touring the city by the day, spending the long nights with the backdrop of a citywide celebration. We understood the exhilaration the Allied soldiers must have felt during World War II after liberating Europe.

Still now, those nights stood out in my heart, making the longing and ache of losing Booth that much more pronounced.

I dug out an old baseball cap and dark glasses from my bag, hoping not to call too much attention to myself. Anwar stopped the Jeep at the top of the hill. "Are you ready?"

I wasn't. Nothing I'd done over the past three years had prepared me for this, but at this point, there could be no turning back. I'd come too far. I needed to know the truth about what had happened to Booth.

Slowly, I nodded and Anwar put the Jeep in gear.

"Once you make it through security, I'll take you to the embassy in Kabul, but no further. They know you will be arriving--they know nothing as to why you are there, only that you are a friend of David's. Keep it that way. Once you've met with the ambassador, you will find a Jeep parked to the south side of the building. The keys are located under the radiator. There are enough supplies to get you where you need to go." He pulled out a piece of paper from his shirt pocket.

"This is the name of a friendly tribesman near Kandahar. You will find him outside the small village of Sandier. He can help you. I trust him. Trust no one else *but* him."

"Thank you," I said humbly. I realized a lot of people were risking their lives to help me find Booth. I owed each of them so much. "Put that somewhere it can't be found," he ordered, ignoring my gratitude. I shoved the piece of paper into a hidden compartment of my bag.

Anwar gave me one final securitizing glance then pulled into the border checkpoint.

The officer was armed with a U.S. made semiautomatic weapon strapped over his shoulder aimed at being threatening. It worked. He recognized Anwar and gave him a little salute. Then he ordered me out of the vehicle and around to an area used for checking luggage. He threw my bag on a table and unzipped it, tossing clothing and personal items everywhere. Surprisingly, with all of the U.S's influences, the security check still didn't possess X-ray, which proved a bonus for my laptop and the weapon I'd hidden inside a false lining.

The guard then snatched my purse and dug through it before tossing it back to me. "Sunglasses."

"I beg your pardon?" I'd tried to perfect the meek persona of a government pencil pusher while using the dark glasses to assess the area.

"Remove your sunglasses and cap," he ordered.

Once I'd done as he asked and he'd stared me down, he tossed my things haphazardly back into the bag and zipped it up. After that, he came around the table.

"Raise your arms." I tried not to be repulsed as he took his time searching my body. I wondered if every person visiting Afghanistan got the same treatment or if it was limited to women.

Resentment for our government still ran deep among local men in spite of the friendly relationship the President of Afghanistan and the U.S. president enjoyed.

He handed me my bag, sunglasses and cap. "You are staying how long?"

"A week." I kept my voice low and flat.

He eyed me suspiciously. "You are on business?"

I shook my head. "No, I'm just visiting your country."

His reaction was unpleasant. He didn't care for Americans. "You will be expected back in one week." With those chilling words, he dismissed me and had a private word with Anwar. My knees were weak and shaking as I got back into the Jeep. The two men laughed and the guard waved at Anwar as he got into the driver's seat.

We made the rest of the short trip to the embassy in silence. I kept glancing over my shoulder, almost certain the guard would change his mind and decide he needed to check my story out more carefully.

"Don't worry," Anwar assured me. "He was easy to buy. He will not have followed you."

I glanced back once more, suppressing a shiver. If the guards were that easy to bribe, then who was to say someone with more money and a greater cause couldn't top Anwar's offer?

Anwar parked the car in front of the embassy on the crowded street. "I can't take you any further. It's too risky for me to be seen with you." He motioned toward the building. "They'll be expecting you." He scribbled a number on a piece of paper. "If you need me, you can reach me here."

I'd promised David I'd stop in at the embassy and let them know I'd arrived and they could pass word back to him. I hated losing the time, but I might need the embassy connection should things turn bad.

I opened the Jeep door and turned to Anwar. "Thank you."

He studied me once more. "Good luck. I hope you find what you're looking for."

Without answering, I walked to the first security checkpoint. It was comforting to see U.S. military officials.

"Yes, ma'am, what is your purpose here today?"

I read the soldier's nametag. "Hello, Officer Blair. I'm Laura Ingalls. I have a meeting with the ambassador here as a courtesy for Ambassador Judah."

He checked his list. "Yes, ma'am. We've been expecting you. Right this way."

I was quickly escorted through the remaining security points by two armed guards. Within seconds, a young woman who appeared to be fresh out of college came and got me from the lobby where I'd been asked to wait.

"Ambassador Khalidid has been expecting you. Ambassador Judah informed us you would be arriving sometime this morning."

"Thank you," I said as I politely followed her down the ancient hallway.

She knocked on a door with the ambassador's name emblazed in gold script and waited until he invited us in.

Once we stepped into the room, the ambassador got to his feet. It appeared as if he'd been going over his schedule with his assistant.

He rounded his desk and took my hand. "It's nice to meet you, Ms. Ingalls. David speaks highly of you." He nodded to my escort and she discreetly left us alone. "Please, sit, sit."

I took the chair he indicated. The young man he'd

been talking with waited until I was seated then introduced himself as Carl Nolan.

The ambassador returned to his seat. "My friend David tells me you are here to do some research on our great city for a book you are working on."

I'd wondered what cover story David would concoct. I fought to keep from smiling at this one. David told me once he retired he planned to write a book about his travels.

"That's correct."

"And you will be staying within the city? Not venturing outside the protection offered here?"

"Yes, that's correct."

"This is good. While Kabul has made great strides in protecting tourists, the desert outside is a different story. Dangerous elements still rule those regions."

I smiled at the ambassador. "I understand. Not to worry, I'll remain in Kabul. Thank you for your time." I got to my feet and headed for the door.

"Carl will show you out."

I left the ambassador with my thanks. The minute we were out of earshot, Carl took me not to my vehicle but to another part of the building.

"You are being watched," he warned.

His words shocked me. What did he know? "I don't know what you are talking about,"

Carl smiled at my answer. "Like you, I once worked for the Agency. Did you think you could cross the border without being spotted? If I know you are here, it won't be long before others do as well."

Although Carl seemed to have my best interest in

mind, I didn't dare let my guard down. "Who besides the *Agency* is watching me?"

"Everyone. Your government. The Afghanistan government. Both sides have reasons for not wanting you to find Agent Tanner."

"What do you mean? What do you know?" He hesitated. "Please, tell me what you know."

His gaze met mine. I could tell he wasn't going to enlighten me. "With the war still being fought in other regions of the country, you have to wonder why a seasoned agent like Tanner was here in this remote area."

Fear and adrenaline cranked to life in the pit of my stomach. "I don't know. Why do you think that is?"

He turned and opened another door that led out to the parking area. "You'll have to ask Agent Tanner that question. If you find him alive."

I left Carl without learning any of the answers I desperately needed. I found the key to the Jeep where Anwar told me it would be. I was literally trembling as I got behind the wheel and cranked the engine to life. I had no idea what I was getting myself into, but there was little time to consider the consequences. I grabbed the map from the glove box and mapped out my route.

Kabul was relatively tame compared to what I'd expected. There were Western influences everywhere. Hotels and restaurants, clothing stores bearing familiar names whizzed by as I headed out of town. I could almost picture Booth's cynical reaction to this. "We liberated these people and now we've turned them into us."

Booth was a firm believer in leaving a country unspoiled. He'd have hated what was happening to this one.

Once I reached the outskirts of the city, I took stock in the supplies. Two full gas cans were strapped to the back of the Jeep. Water, energy bars, cookies, and some dried fruit stashed beneath a blanket. Everything was as Anwar had said. I slipped the Glock from its hiding place in my bag and tucked it under the seat of the Jeep, then headed toward the mountains that loomed in the distance.

Kandahar was located some ways from Kabul, although the flat, open terrain surrounding me now made it hard to judge distances. Everything looked closer than it was.

I'd traveled only a few miles when a small village appeared in the desert heat. Best to skirt the place and not take any undue risks. I grabbed the binoculars from the glove box and focused on the village. No one seemed to be anywhere around, in spite of the fact that it was still relatively early.

Many of the villages nearby had suffered damage in the U.S. air strikes involved in searching for Bin Laden and the Taliban after. Some had been rebuilt. This one had not.

Still, there was no need to take chances. I headed out to the right of the village at a safe distance. If anyone were still around, it would probably not be the type of person I'd want to encounter.

The heat in the desert had to be close to a hundred. I took off my shirt, grateful that I'd remembered to wear a thin T-shirt beneath.

This was no-man's-land. The Afghanistan government had no control here. Tribal law ruled. After a while, I passed a couple of nomads traveling with camels in tow. They seemed uninterested in me. Apparently, they were used to strangers in their land. Or maybe keeping a low profile was all that kept them alive.

I searched beneath the blanket until I came up with a package of cookies. Not exactly the best meal, but it would do for the time being.

By my best calculations, I'd reach Kandahar before nightfall, where I'd skirt the city and head north to the area where Booth was last heard from. The thought of sleeping in the desert with only the Jeep for protection did little for my peace of mind. Enemies of the U.S. were everywhere out here. Take your pick. Taliban, al-Qaeda, ISIS, unfriendly tribesmen, not to mention a few desert creatures that could be as lethal as any carefully placed bomb.

A little past twilight, the lights of Kandahar came into view. The city was closed off, sprawling, and like most cities here, built low to the ground. Parts of it had been destroyed in past air strikes and recently rebuilt. Still today, the Taliban had Kandahar in a stranglehold. In spite of all our efforts to eradicate their threat, large pockets of Taliban lived openly in the city, along with what was rumored to be some of the FBI's top most wanted terrorists.

* * * *

"You want to tell me why someone matching Rachel Weiss' description crossed the border into Afghanistan?"

Director Hughes' angry denouncement hit Michael out of left field. It was the last thing he expected to hear.

"What? That's impossible. I have people sitting on her. I spoke to them minutes earlier. She's at the embassy."

"She's not. You screwed up. She lost your tail. Someone using a fake ID by the name of Laura Ingalls crossed into Kabul three hours ago."

Michael smiled in spite of the gravity of the situation. Laura Ingalls Wilder was Rachel's favorite childhood author.

"You're off this thing," Hughes informed him and he knew exactly what that meant. Someone would be sent to bring Rachel back. It didn't particularly matter how. He couldn't let it happen.

Michael was in for a battle. Hughes knew too much about his past connection to her. "Director Hughes, I've got this thing. Let me handle it."

"You don't have it. It's out of control and we can't afford this now."

"I can contain her. Let me handle it."

For a moment, he thought Hughes might refuse flat out. "You've got twenty-four hours," the director spat out. "Then I'm taking over."

"I'll need more time. She's got a head start."

"Twenty-four hours and then I'll handle it my way."

Hughes slammed the phone in Michael's ear to get his point across.

Things were getting way out of control. This was supposed to have been an easy mission and yet Booth was missing and Rachel had gotten herself into something that might cost her life.

His first call was to Sam. "Call the team in Jerusalem off."

"What? Why? They still have the Weiss woman under surveillance."

"They don't. She slipped their tail. I told you she was good. She's in Afghanistan. Get a team together there, get her picture out to them, and tell them she's using the name Laura Ingalls. Hurry. She'll be halfway to Kandahar by now."

"Will do."

"Oh, and Sam, meet me at the airport. Have the jet ready to fly in half an hour."

"Where are you going?"

"Not me...us. *We're* going to Kandahar. We're going to handle this thing personally. I can't afford any more screw ups."

Chapter Four

As a known enemy holdout, Kandahar would be locked up tight with guards posted everywhere around the city. Skirting an area that size without being noticed wouldn't be easy. The Jeep's fuel gauge was almost in the red. Luckily, refueling wasn't going to be a problem.

I found an outgrowth of rock and filled the tank, keeping a careful eye toward the city. Maneuvering around Kandahar would cost me an additional hour's time. Once I was out of the area, the mountains would be some twenty kilometers beyond. I'd been watching them grow like shadows in the distance for hours.

With the setting sun, the temperature of the desert plunged quickly. I retrieved the down jacket from the backseat and put it on.

I'd brought my personal cell phone along and on impulse decided to check it. I found another text communication from my mystery number. Its message consisted of one word. *Bel-Ahzar.*

I had no idea what Bel-Ahzar was meant to convey.

On impulse, I got out the map and studied it carefully. Bel-Ahzar was a small village at the base of Mount Morieh. Was someone trying to tell me where I could find Booth, or was I walking into a trap?

Whatever the answer, I knew I had to go there.

I typed a quick reply.

Who are you and what do you know about Booth Tanner?

My answer might be hours in the making, if at all.

The sky above filled with stars. I killed the Jeep's lights. There was a perfect full moon hanging low along the desert's horizon. I made my way slowly around Kandahar's perimeter by moonlight.

When I reached the first of the foothills, I put the Jeep into four-wheel drive. As I climbed slowly along the rocky terrain, my phone signaled an incoming message.

I've seen him. He's still alive. If you want to know more, you'll come to Bel-Ahzar. My name is Rahab.

Abruptly, I braked the Jeep. Obviously, the name was a fake. There was a passage in the Bible where a woman named Rahab had hidden the Jewish men sent to spy out the stronghold, Jericho. Was this person trying to indicate they were friendly to my cause or was this another ruse?

Fearing a trap, I dug out the name of the tribesman Anwar had given me.

His name was Khalid Assaid. Anwar had told me that Khalid was a nomad whose dwelling could be found north of Kandahar at the base of the mountains. I decided I couldn't risk traveling any further in the dark. With the city behind me, the mountainous terrain continued to grow treacherous. I had no idea what danger waited me out here in the open or who might be coming after me. By now, I was pretty certain Michael would know where I was.

At any given time, there would be a team of CIA agents in the area. All it would take was one call.

I pulled the Jeep behind a protruding rock at the foot of a hill. Because I so needed the courage to go on, I pulled out my pocket Bible and read my favorite passage in Deuteronomy 31:6

Be strong and of a good courage, fear not, nor be afraid of them: for the LORD thy God, he it is that doth go with thee; he will not fail thee, nor forsake thee

When I finished reading the verses, I tried to sleep. But rest was next to impossible with all the questions scurrying around in my head. I allowed myself a few minutes to close my eyes and rest. Though I'd been out of the game for a long time, my instincts were still sharp. I automatically woke every fifteen minutes.

As always, my thoughts were on my daughter. At two, she was still too young to wonder about her father. Of course, the day would come when I would have to try to explain the truth. Would she resent me for not allowing her father to be part of her life?

Father, please no.

I could take just about anything but losing my daughter's love. Since leaving Booth, she'd been the only thing to keep me going.

"Who are you?" A heavily accented voice intruded into my dream.

My eyes shot open at the sound of it and I clutched the weapon I'd hidden beneath my right leg.

It was still dark out and the Jeep was surrounded by some ten men, dressed like nomads. A tall, thin Arab with aged eyes stood in front, holding a gun to my head. I froze.

The gun dug into my left temple. "Again, who are you and why are you here?" The men, although armed, appeared to be herdsmen. I took a chance they wouldn't be Taliban soldiers in disguise.

"I'm looking for Khalid Assaid." The man holding the weapon didn't react to my answer.

All I could see was his dark eyes. "And why are you looking for this Khalid? Who sent you?"

I hadn't moved a muscle. My fingers still circled the weapon. "My friend, Anwar. He told me I could trust Khalid."

After another minute of watching me carefully, sizing me up, the man motioned for one of his men to get me out of the Jeep.

The younger man grabbed my arm and I jerked free and leveled the weapon at him. "That's far enough."

I'd clearly shocked them, which worked to my advantage. The man reaching for me looked to the leader.

After a moment, the leader smiled in satisfaction.

"Ah, you are the one."

I glanced from the man closest to me to the leader, never lowering the Glock. "What are you talking about?"

"Anwar told me you could take care of yourself. I didn't believe him. I told him no Western woman could handle herself under these conditions. Apparently, I was wrong." He lowered his weapon and held out his hand. "I am Khalid Assaid, at your service. Now, if you would do me the honor of returning the favor and lowering your weapon before you kill my nephew, I would be much relieved."

Adrenaline pumped through my body like an alcohol rush. My hands shook as I lowered the weapon and got out of the Jeep.

I took Khalid's hand and shook it, then almost gave it all away by giving him my real name. "Laura Ingalls," I stammered instead.

Khalid bowed slightly. "You are in a dangerous area. You are lucky I was the one who found you first. The Taliban control most of this region. They have my people by their throats. If you will come with me, our camp is over that hill. Follow me, please."

I got back into the Jeep and waited while the men mounted their horses. Then we made our way at a fast click to their camp.

By the time we reached the camp, the sun had begun to lighten the sky. There were woman and children milling around the camp as I climbed out of the Jeep. They watched me with open suspicion. I wondered what type of life they led in the midst of this unending war.

Khalid escorted me to a tent. A moment later, a woman arrived carrying strong coffee. Once she'd left, he poured some and handed it to me. "Now, tell me how

I can help you, Laura Ingalls."

I glanced up and found he was grinning. I realized he'd seen right through my fake name. I lifted my chin and said, "You can tell me what you know about the village of Bel-Ahzar."

The amusement drained from Khalid's dark eyes. "A dangerous place to be for the strongest of men. For a woman, it would be suicide."

"I don't have a choice." I pulled out the picture of Booth I'd tucked away in my pocket and handed him the photo. "I'm looking for this man. I have reason to believe he may be in Bel-Ahzar."

Khalid studied the photo of Booth then glanced at me. "CIA?"

I debated how much to expose to him. Giving away an agent's history to an unknown was like violating the first commandment. Booth had drilled that rule into me from the beginning. Unfortunately, I needed Khalid's help too much to keep Booth's secrets. "That's right," I admitted.

"And you? Who are you besides a friend of Anwar? CIA?"

I shook my head. "No. I'm a friend of this man. I have reason to believe he may be in danger."

"If he's in Bel-Ahzar, I'd be willing to bet on it. The Taliban use it as a prison camp. They have many Americans there."

The image of the torture Booth would be subject to was hard to take. "There are others there? How many?"

Khalid shook his head. "I said they use it as a prison. The ones taken to Bel-Ahzar rarely come out alive."

My knees deserted me and I sank to the ground. "Can you help me?"

He watched me for several seconds without any sign of emotion, then spread his hands in front of him. "Not like this. I would be signing both of our death sentences if I went there with someone who cannot control their emotions."

I struggled to wipe the fear from my face. "You're wrong. I can control my emotions. Please, I need your help."

He wasn't convinced. After a moment, he asked, "Why do you think he is in Bel-Ahzar?"

I told him about the text messages I'd received from the alias Rahab.

"I see. How do you know this isn't a trap? I can imagine someone associated with the CIA would have many enemies. As would someone who is a friend of the CIA," he added quietly.

"I don't know that it isn't a trap. I only have a name. Rahab. It's not much, I know."

"Not much at all," he agreed. "But I will help you because I believe you, but only if you do exactly as I tell you. A woman traveling there alone will be taken into custody immediately. With the proper clothing, you could pass for a young man."

Relief overwhelmed me. "Thank you. When can we leave?"

He continued to watch me before answering. "Soon. We will need to take some of my men with us. I often travel there to buy supplies. We will not draw undue attention. You will not speak. Not ever. If anyone asks me, you are my nephew. Do you understand?"

"Yes," I smiled with relief. "Thank you."

"One more thing. You will leave your weapon along with your ID here. If you are searched, you must be without them."

The thought of leaving my weapon behind left me feeling exposed, but I needed Khalid's help so I'd do what he asked. "I understand."

"Good. Drink up. We will leave immediately. I take it you can ride?"

I'd been on a horse only once in my life, but I didn't tell Khalid this. "Yes, of course."

He eyed me suspiciously and then seemed to decide I was telling the truth. "All right, I will have my wife bring you something to wear."

Khalid left and a few minutes later, the same woman as before entered the tent. She carried a tray of food and a stack of clothes.

"Thank you," I managed to say to her back as she left me alone without a word.

I ate the food with more of an appetite than I imagined. It had been hours since I'd had a decent meal.

With the food gone, I changed quickly into the clothing. When I left the tent, I found Khalid waiting next to the opening. He looked me up and down, then adjusted my turban so that it partially covered my face, and grunted in satisfaction.

"I have a gentle mount for you. Again, I must caution you, no matter what happens, don't speak to anyone. Your accent alone will give you away. Your use of the dialect will only confirm it. Do as I say and with any luck, you'll be okay."

Four more men joined us. One was Khalid's nephew. We set out for a mountain range in the distance. We'd traveled less than half an hour when the desert sun began to beat down on us. The heat was unbearable, making the loose fitting robes cling like paste to my body.

We topped another hill when a small, run-down village came into sight. Bel-Ahzar.

Khalid slowed his mount and waited for me to catch up. "Remember, keep your mouth shut. If this goes bad, I'll do my best to help, but you must get out of there by any means possible."

We entered the village at a slow canter. Though it was still quite early, there were dozens of men milling around. Several eyed us suspiciously. I knew without asking that these men were my sworn enemy.

I tried to think of how I would ever find the person known as Rahab. I assumed she was female, but there were few women about. Of those I could see, all were escorted by men.

Khalid reined his horse to a halt. He dismounted and indicated that I should do the same.

"Follow me and try to act like a man," he whispered against my ear. Our arrival had not seemed to draw too much unwanted attention. Several men appeared to know Khalid.

We made our way to a small open market filled with freshly skinned animals, fowls and various strange looking vegetables and grains. The men that came with us examined the goods. I stuck close to Khalid's side.

"How do we find Rahab?" I whispered and Khalid

threw me an angry look.

"I have an idea. You will keep quiet, please."

Khalid stopped in front of a merchant selling vegetables. It was clear that they knew each other well.

Once they'd exchanged a few pleasantries, the merchant became curious about me. Khalid said something to him and he laughed. After a few more friendly exchanges, Khalid brought up the name Rahab.

The merchant gestured wildly in the direction of a less than savory section of the village.

Khalid nodded, then indicated that I should follow. When we were out of earshot, Khalid said that a woman of ill repute named Rahab lived on the outskirts of the village.

"We don't have much time. We will be drawing attention to ourselves by being in that part of the village," he said with distaste.

Trying to be as discreet as possible, we found ourselves standing in front of a shabby mud-hewn hut.

"This is it?" I asked in amazement, forgetting that I wasn't supposed to speak. Khalid didn't answer. He knocked on the door and a woman dressed in dark garb appeared in the doorway.

Khalid spoke to her briefly. She gestured for us to come inside. Once we were in, she locked the door, then disappeared into another part of the house.

"What did she say to you? Is she Rahab?"

Khalid shook his head. "No, but she claims to know this person and can get a message to her. I don't like the sound of this."

"Where did she go?"

Khalid put his finger to his lips to indicate I should be quiet. The woman returned a few seconds later and spoke again to Khalid.

After another rapid exchange of conversation, Khalid indicated we should leave.

I waited until we were outside of the house to question him. "What did she say, Khalid?"

He stopped a few feet in front and turned to look back at me. "We need to go. Now. It isn't safe here any longer."

"No. Not until you tell what happened in there."

He glanced around us. What few people there were didn't seem the least bit interested in what we were doing.

"She said that Rahab will arrange a meeting between us tonight. That you are to come alone. You are being set up. No doubt your friend is dead."

His words were like a knife to my heart. I blew out a breath, fighting back emotions I'd hoped were dead. "No. I won't accept that. I can't."

Khalid reached for my arm to stop me, his face inches from mine. "And if you go there tonight alone, you won't come out alive."

"Maybe. But I have to know the truth."

Khalid let me go, glanced away, then all around us before heading for the market, leaving me no other option but to follow. Khalid's men were waiting for us next to our mounts.

We traveled the rest of the journey in silence. Once we'd returned to the camp and dismounted, Khalid indicated that his nephew and I should follow him back inside his tent. I retrieved my phone and found a message from Rahab. I was to meet her at eight at a place called The Well of Jacob.

I told Khalid this.

"I cannot guarantee your safety or the safety of my men if you go there. My gut instinct tells me you will be walking into a trap."

I believed the same thing. In fact, I was beginning to get suspicious as to how someone had found out about my relationship to Booth in the first place. Only a handful of people knew we'd once been lovers. All were supposed to be on our side of this battle.

"Probably. But if there is a chance he's still alive I have to try."

"Have you ever considered someone might be using him to get to you? The time for secrets is past. I must know what your connection is to this man."

I had considered this, but why would someone be after me? I hadn't been part of the game in a long time. Sure, I'd made enemies. But I'd left that world behind. Why would someone wait so long to come after me?

As next in line to take the controls of a volatile region, I was forced to admit, I could have been the target all along. Maybe Booth was a means to the end. *Father, please don't let him have died because of me.*

"You are CIA, like this man?"

I met Khalid's gaze before answering. "I was."

He gave a short nod. "The Well of Jacob is an open area in the desert some ten kilometers from here. There is no place to hide. Simply open desert. If we go with you, we will be spotted right away. I see one of two things happening. The person you are meeting will be spooked and leave if this is a legitimate meet. Or my team will be annihilated. Neither scenario is pleasant, do you think?"

Khalid was right. This risk far outweighed the gain. If the meet were legit, what did I hope to learn? That Booth might still be alive. I couldn't wait for Michael to send help. The CIA had written Booth off. If the situation were reversed, Booth would do the same for me no matter how much it cost him or how badly we'd parted.

"No, you're right, but I have to go. I have to help him."

Khalid's guarded stare scrutinized my facial expression for answers. "This is about more than completing a mission, isn't it? You have a personal connection to this man."

It wasn't a question and I didn't try to deny it. "Yes." That he didn't approve was easy to read. Khalid got to his feet and paced the tent, anger following at the heels of every step.

"You're willing to risk my men's lives along with your own to save him?"

I owed Khalid the truth. "No, I can't ask you to put your men at risk. But I will do whatever it takes. If it means I must put my life in jeopardy to save the life of my daughter's father, then I'll do it." Emotionally drained, the familiar stirring of tears returned. I hadn't cried since my baby's birth. Being back in this situation of life and death, risking everything once again, and knowing it might all turn out to be in vain because Booth might already be dead, brought back a barrage of unwelcome emotions. "Booth is my husband and he has a daughter he doesn't know anything about. I owe him...something. I owe her more."

Khalid stopped and watched me incredulously. "This man has no idea that he has a child?"

I shook my head, regretting I'd shared this personal information with a virtual stranger.

After a moment, Khalid said, "All right. I will help you. But we can only go so far with you. You will be on your own for the meet."

He found a map and spread it out before us on a small table, jabbing a finger at a particular section. "Here. There's a small outcropping of rocks here. My men and I will follow you as far as this point. We'll wait for you there. You will stay in touch every moment of the way beyond this point. If anything looks suspicious, you will leave immediately. Do you understand?"

I nodded. "Yes. Yes, I understand."

Khalid's dark gaze inspected me once more, not liking what he saw. "You should get some rest. The heat of the desert can be overpowering to those unaccustomed to it. My wife will bring you something to eat and then you will rest. I will explain to my men what is happening."

Without another word, he left me alone. As before, his wife returned with food and coffee, barely sparing me a glance. I wondered what thoughts she might be keeping to herself. The things she would have seen here in this barren desert land would shock most Western women. I gratefully accepted the meal she offered.

Finding sleep when my thoughts spun and my body hummed with energy was not easy to come by.

There was a real chance I might be walking into a death trap tonight and I prayed, for my daughter's sake, I would live to tell of this day.

Although I was taking a huge risk someone might be tracking my calls, I missed Ava terribly and needed to hear her sweet voice once more as a reminder as to why I was here in the first place.

I called Dana's cell number. She picked up after the second ring. "Rachel? Oh thank God, I've been worried."

"I know. Dana, I can't talk long. I'm okay. I'm still searching for the problem. Is Ava up?"

It was my daughter's naptime, but I had to take the chance. "I put her down for her nap a few minutes ago, but she'll be mad at me if I don't wake her. She'll want to talk to you."

"No, Dana, don't do that..." Too late, I realized Dana was no longer listening. I heard her saying something and then my daughter's voice came on the line.

"Mommy!" My daughter's excited voice came through the phone loud and clear making me question everything I was risking by being here and bringing new tears to my eyes.

"Hi there, baby."

"Mommy, when are you coming home? I miss you."

I fought back a sob. I couldn't let my daughter hear my fear. "I miss you too, baby. I'll be home as soon as I can. Are you behaving yourself for Dana, Uncle David, and Aunt Hannah?"

"Um hum. Uncle David said he would take me to the zoo on Friday."

"That's terrific." Friday was three days away. Would I be back in time to join my daughter and David for their excursion? I had no idea what awaited me or if I'd be able to find out the truth in Booth's disappearance.

"Baby, I have to go now. You be good and I'll see you soon. I love you, Ava."

"Love you too, Mommy."

After I disconnected the call, I sank to my knees. Here alone in a place that represented the enemy to my country, my nationality, and me, I desperately needed God. Now, like so many times in the past with Jewish history, I prayed to God for deliverance.

Chapter Five

"Anything yet?" The flight to Kabul had seemed endless. Valuable time had been wasted in the air, but there was nothing to be done about it. This thing was too important to leave in the hands of others. Michael needed to be personally involved in this one.

A team of CIA agents had met their plane. They'd been discreetly escorted to a waiting Suburban fitted for traveling in the harsh desert terrain.

"We have two agents working undercover in Kandahar. There's been no sighting there of Tanner or the woman as of yet, but the team should be arriving in the area where Tanner went missing any moment," the senior agent said before he spared Michael a glance and returned to his steely surveillance of the airport layout. It was impossible to read his expression through the mirrored sunglasses, but Michael knew it by heart. This was bad for business. The resentment of American involvement in Afghanistan's political affairs was still strong. If word of Booth's covert activities were to reach the government's opposing party, the virtual powder keg they were sitting on would erupt into all-out civil war.

Michael turned to his partner. "Sam, did you find out where the text message originated yet?"

"My team's still working it. We should have something in a few more hours."

"Light a fire under them, will you? We don't have any time to spare."

Sam fished out his cell phone and checked for messages. "We have something. They've tracked it to the mountain region close to where Booth went missing. A village by the name of Bel-Ahzar." Sam glanced at Michael. "Ever heard of it?"

With great effort, he managed to be convincing. "No. But it's as good a place to start as any, though." He addressed his next question to the senior agent, Sheridan. "How soon before you can get us there?"

Agent Sheridan looked to the driver to confirm.

"Couple of hours, sir."

Michael settled back against the seat without answering and let the memories of her return. Rahab. He hadn't wanted to think of her again. She was still alive. He wasn't sure how he felt about that. There was a time when hearing her name made him long to be with her. Their romance had ignited like a firestorm that one brief summer. It ended when rumors of Rahab's loyalties came into question.

Had she become a double agent as suspected by those closest to Booth? If so, had he, Michael, sent his friend to his death? Would he find Booth alive or had Rahab betrayed more than Michael's trust? Had she betrayed Booth and her country? That was the problem with using local operatives, even the ones you thought you knew. You never knew which way their loyalty might blow. Michael hadn't told Rachel, but he'd been Booth's handler and the one to have the final say as to whether Booth went on this mission. And as Booth's handler, Michael had cautioned him against trusting Rahab too much. Still, if Booth was wounded, as Michael believed, then he might not have had a choice in confiding in her.

Agent Sheridan's monotone voice interrupted his thoughts. "We'll be there by eight. We'll have to proceed carefully. At the very least, the village is under the control of the Taliban."

"What's the worst scenario?" Michael asked.

"ISIS. Al-Qaeda."

Michael understood the drill although he wasn't a field agent. He'd handled some of the best, Booth included. They'd need to have a contact to get them inside. He'd need to get to Rahab before the rest of his team if he was going to try and contain this thing.

How had he let this get out of control? "You have someone in mind?" Michael asked.

"I do," Sheridan assured him with bravado.

The fewer details he and Sam knew about the contact, the less they'd be able to reveal if it came to that. Where they were heading, there was a real threat of capture. Here in no-man's-land, anything was possible.

The team lapsed into silence. Michael opened his

laptop and pretended to work, his thoughts going back over the final moments and his last conversation with Booth before he'd gone radio silent.

Booth hadn't been himself for a while. His last call had only served to emphasize the point. He'd seemed depressed. He talked about coming home to the States. Michael had wondered about the reason behind Booth's sudden need to be on American soil. He still remembered Booth's answer, though vague. He'd said he needed to find something back home worth believing in to make all of the things they were doing in the name of justice worth the price. At the time, Michael'd thought Booth was battle weary. Now, he wasn't sure.

He still remembered the promise he'd made to Booth to keep him there. Once this mission was finished, he'd bring Booth home. He hadn't meant it and he figured Booth had guessed as much, but it had been enough to keep him focused for a while. And he needed Booth's focused attention. The stakes were too high.

Now, after almost a week of silence, Michael feared the worst. If Booth were still alive, he'd find a way to get word to him.

Michael had lost track of the regrets. He knew sending Booth into this particular area with only a local operative as backup was risky, but the reward if Booth were successful--and Booth was the only person who could make this mission happen--would be enormous.

Capturing al-Qaeda second in command alive could bring them within striking distance of breaking the back of one of the largest terrorist cells and almost guarantee a huge win in the war of terror.

Now, with Booth missing, the trail had gone from cold to non-existent.

"You okay?"

Michael stirred himself from his thoughts. Sam obviously had been trying to get his attention for a while. "Yes, of course."

"You're sure?" Sam was a good man, but this was his first mission abroad. He wouldn't be learning from the master. Under Booth's tutelage, Sam could have been one of the best. No other agent in the field had Booth's skills and intuition. Instead, Sam would be stuck with learning the ropes from men like Sheridan and himself, people who were little more than pencil pushers for the agency.

"Yeah, sure, what's up?"

Sam lowered his voice. "We have a hit on Rachel's phone. She placed a call less than two hours earlier from here."

Michael closed the laptop and sat up straighter. "Where?"

"Satellite link has it less than three kilometers from Bel-Ahzar."

"She's going after our woman there. I need to know if there's been any new contact between this Rahab and Rachel."

Sam glanced discreetly around the vehicle's interior. "I checked. Two messages."

"Can you get me their context?"

Michael knew what Sam's answer would be. "I'd need a court order for that."

"This is a matter of national security. Do it. I'll deal

with the consequences should they arise."

"Okay. It could take a while."

Michael turned away, glancing out the window as night descended rapidly on the desert outside the Suburban.

He had less than half a day's time to fix this thing before Hughes' paranoia took over and he put the command out to take care of Rachel--and Booth, if he was still alive.

His last hope was the man still had something resembling a moral conscience left in him. The only thing Hughes was guilty of thus far was sanctioning the covert mission that had possibly cost Booth his life. If he followed through with what he'd threatened, he'd be guilty of murder. Unfortunately, Michael had no solid proof and Hughes was good at covering up or burying evidence.

* * * *

"You always did look good in jeans. They show your softer side, unlike those stiff business suits you're always wearing. And you do have a softer side, Rachel, no matter how hard you try to deny it these days." He still looked the same. As he had that final night three years earlier. His smile still possessed the power to draw me to him like a moth to flame. Charming and annoying.

"Booth. Dear God, Booth." I breathed in the familiar scent of him. I touched his face, my fingers stroking the scraggly stubble that shadowed the hard planes of his cheek. I knew every line, all the dimensions

of him.

He closed his eyes and nuzzled warm lips again my hand. His feel--alive, electrical. Reassuring. Then as quickly as it emerged, his smile disappeared. Booth suddenly grew serious. I'd seen that look before. He was here to warn me of something.

"You shouldn't have come here."

"Why? What are you involved in, Booth?"

"You're in danger here, Rach. You're out of practice. You can't help me, Rach. Let me go."

"No, I can't. Booth, I have to help you for--"

"Our daughter needs you. Go home to her. Now. Tonight. Before it's too late. Don't go out there tonight."

My next breath lodged in my throat at the mention of Ava. He knew about Ava. "How did you know?"

His image dimmed. His hand on my shoulder turned colder as he shook me hard. "I'm dead, Rachel. I know because I'm dead."

In an instant, I awoke. Fear and adrenaline propelled me into a sitting position. In those first cloudy minutes between the clarity of the dream and reality, I could almost believe Booth was real. Almost. Until I spotted Khalid standing next to the bed, watching me with what was quickly becoming a familiar look of concern.

I forced myself to speak. Try to appeal normal but the racing of my pulse had to be evident to anyone within five feet of me.

"What time is it?" I pushed the words out.

After a lengthy expanse of time, he chose to answer me. "Late. The moon will be rising soon. I've been trying to wake you for a while. We should go."

I swung my feet to the ground. "I'm ready. Let's do this."

Khalid's hand was firm on my arm. "Are you? I wonder. Do not make me regret this decision, Laura Ingalls."

He turned on one booted heel and left me silently watching him go.

* * * *

Khalid reined in his mount once we reached the outcropping of rocks close to The Well of Jacob.

"You have the phone on silent?" he asked for the third time.

"Yes." I knew his concern was for me as well as his men.

"You know what to do?"

I nodded. "Yes."

Khalid and his team would remain here, hidden within the shelter of the rock formation. With any luck, no one had been close enough to witness our arrival.

"I'll be fine. I can handle myself. If this thing goes south, you need to get your people out of here as quickly as possible."

While he agreed, I knew better. Khalid would be there for me at risk of his life.

When the men were in position, I nudged the mare's flanks and she began a slow canter.

Still in the protective shelter of the rocks, I pulled out the night vision binoculars and trained them in the direction of the well. Someone was there.

I'd tucked my Glock inside a hidden pocket of my jacket. Its cold metal somehow comforting.

As I moved in close to the well the person leaning against it still hadn't moved. I reined the mare to a halt and dismounted with weapon drawn.

"Rahab?"

The woman dressed in dark clothing from head to toe didn't move. Piercing fear and adrenaline swept through me like a slug of alcohol. I hit the talk button on the phone and dialed the number Khalid gave me before creeping close enough to feel for a pulse. The moment I touched her she toppled over. She was dead.

I had just enough time to see that the woman's throat had been slashed.

Then I heard a noise behind me. As I turned, a heavy object hammered against my left temple. Then blackness.

* * * *

He took my hand and led me a little way from the rest of the team. Something troubled him tonight. I could see it in him.

"Booth, what is it?" I shivered at the lost look on his face. I'd never seen him so serious before.

He stared into my eyes for the longest time then shook his head leaving me with the feeling that something important had been left unsaid.

Booth drew me into his strong embrace and I went willingly in spite of the strain that existed between us. I still loved him after all.

He held me close and we stared up at a multitude of stars above. The desert held its own form of magic and the night should have been perfect, but I couldn't let go of my fears.

"What's troubling you, Booth," I asked again because I had to know. I desperately wanted him to share his thoughts with me.

He watched me for the longest time before he drew me closer and kissed me like only Booth could. Had it been my imagination or had I really heard him whisper, "I love you"? I stopped and stared up at him, but nothing showed. Regret was hard to swallow. Booth couldn't give me his heart because it belonged to the job. I'd known this and accepted it in the beginning. I couldn't any longer.

"I should go back first. We don't want the rest of the team getting ideas." He tried to make a joke, but there was something in his voice that sounded sad.

Once he left me, I didn't return to camp right away. I couldn't, because if felt as if my heart had shattered into a thousand pieces.

* * * *

I opened my eyes with difficulty and felt the sting of bittersweet tears close by. I remembered the time in the desert with Booth as if it were yesterday. The heartache, the love I felt for him was still there in my heart. In spite of everything he'd put me through, I missed him terribly and I'd give just about anything for one more moment with him.

Excruciating pain shot down the left side of my face. I winced and tried to focus. All around me was a thick darkness that seemed to seep inside my head. And cold. The air was heavy with a musty smell and something familiar and foul. Death.

I realized I was standing. My hands tied above my head tight enough that the circulation had left them. I tried to move them and pins and needles shot down my arms.

The darkness around me was impenetrable. I couldn't see an inch in front of me. Surprisingly, my feet were not bound. I tentatively moved one. I appeared to be standing on something concrete. I extended my foot as far as I could reach but didn't find an end. I was in a building, possibly a bunker. I had no idea how big my prison cell was or how deep it might be buried.

Behind me, something scurried and I fought the urge to scream.

Panic welled from deep inside of me. With all my strength, I forced it down, training my mind back over the things that I knew. Best to concentrate on facts and not let my imagination run rampant.

The person I believed to be Rahab was dead. I'd managed to get a call off to Khalid, but it had not been in time to save me from the trap I'd walked into.

I could only hope the signal had gotten through and that Khalid would come for me. Hopefully, he would have some idea where I'd been taken. I prayed he wasn't in on it all along.

I stretched my fingers as far as I could reach and tried to determine the type of restraints I was up against. A thick rope bound my hands.

My head throbbed from the blow I'd sustained. I wondered how long I'd been unconscious. Hours? Days?

Please, God, no. The longer I'd been missing without an attempt at being rescued, the greater my chance of not walking out of this thing.

I tried to keep my fear in check. Panicking now would almost guarantee death. I took a deep breath and remembered the things I'd learned from Booth about survival. I wasn't a rookie. I'd been in this situation once before. But that time I'd had Booth's expertise to get me through. First and foremost was the need to know my surroundings. I listened to the subtle sounds around me, trying to sift through the overwhelming silence and pick up something that might give me an idea of where I was being held.

Instinct told me it would be an underground bunker. If I'd been right and I'd managed to place the call to Khalid, then whoever took me would have known how to disappear quickly. Khalid and his team would have been there within five minutes tops. I'd panned the surrounding area with my night vision goggles and hadn't seen another outcropping of rocks. No other building. Only desert. Somehow, there had to be an entrance in the desert to this place. Would Khalid suspect the same? I could only pray he would.

I listened to the scurrying sound behind me. It sounded as if rats were moving around on something.

Boxes maybe?

The place smelled dank and sour, like rotting fruit. I twisted around so I could get a 360-degree view, but nothing but darkness could be seen. I froze in place at the sound of footsteps nearby. More than one set, judging from the sound of it. I could hear their quiet bits of conversation. Arabic. While I understood the language, they were just far enough away so that I understood only every fifth word or so.

The sound of someone fiddling with a lock above and to the left of me, then the sound of rusty hinges protesting as they were forced to open.

A piercing beam of a flashlight momentarily blinded me. But not before they saw that I was awake.

One of them spoke, eliciting laughter from his cohorts. The flashlight never left my eyes. Someone stepped close and yanked my head back. I could feel the sharp edge of a knife nick at my throat.

My assailant said something to the others. My Arabic was rusty, but I'd picked up enough to know my fate. They wouldn't kill me yet. They needed information. The knife dug deeper into my neck. At this point, I was almost certain the fate I'd be forced to suffer would make my death seem like a welcome release.

* * * *

"She's...gone? Where? How?" Michael wasn't sure he'd understood the tribesman's dialect clearly enough. After being told about the botched meet, Michael insisted the team divert to the location. They'd arrived in time to see total chaos unfold.

Someone had killed Rahab. Slashed her throat from one end to the other. Michael swallowed back regret as he looked at the woman he'd once loved. That piece of truth was best left buried in their pasts.

One of the local agents traveling with Sheridan's team knew the tribesmen living in the region.

"They've worked for us in the past. We can trust them," Sheridan assured him. At this point, Michael wondered if there was anyone in this God forsaken land who could be trusted.

The nomads searching the area had acted as Rachel's backup. They'd left her alone for less than a handful of minutes and she'd vanished into thin air. The leader, a tall and deceptively thin man with cunningly sharp eyes and known as Khalid acknowledged Michael's question with a slight bow of his head. "That is correct. Whoever took her may still be close, I believe. With miles and miles of desert, what we are looking for will be like searching for a needle. Especially at night."

"Then why'd you let her come here in the first place? You had to have known the outcome?" Michael fired back the question only to have it met with stony silence.

Angering the tribesman was a bad move on his part. Khalid and his men were vital to the operation. Calling for backup at this point would be ridiculously slow. "I'm sorry. No one's blaming you. We appreciate your help. Tell us what you need."

"Do you have flashlights?" Khalid asked after another stony beat passed between them.

Sheridan affirmed with a brief nod.

"Then we need to search the desert floor. We're looking for an underground entrance. If we're lucky, we might be able to find their footsteps still in the sand. But time is running out. The wind has picked up. We have only a matter of minutes left to find any trace of them."

Michael nodded to Sheridan. "Make it happen, now."

The team of tribesmen and agents searched more than an hour without any luck.

"This is pointless," Michael admitted at last. "We'll need to wait until morning. I'll call for more men to help with the search."

Khalid reluctantly agreed. "All right. We'll camp here. I'll send one of my men back for help as well." He dispatched one of the younger tribesmen, a relative, giving the order to take his own mount, a sleek black stallion that looked faster than the night.

With the man riding at breakneck speed into the distance, Khalid turned back to Michael. "Maybe you can tell me why this woman was out here in the first place. When the man she is searching for's own team has left him here to die."

Michael took his time answering. He couldn't reveal too much to this man. He'd been almost relieved by the news of Rahab's death though her memories were not all troubled ones. Now Rachel was gone, possibly dead and his chances of containing this thing grew more distant with each new death.

"You've clearly worked with our government in the past. You know what's at stake. You know sometimes sacrifices have to be made for the greater good. The man Laura is searching for was here to kill someone. Someone big."

Khalid watched him without speaking. The man had perfected the stare down. It was certainly working on Michael. "And now he is missing. This woman is dead and someone else might be soon. Is this someone big worth it?"

Michael's gaze never wavered from Khalid. "Yes. For my people as well as yours."

The silence following Michael's declaration made it clear what Khalid's opinion would be.

"You're thinking they've taken her underground?" Michael forged on. He didn't care about Khalid's opinions. He cared less for his judgment. He *needed* a plan. Needed to get Rachel back and prayed this wasn't the work of his own people.

"Yes. There are virtual miles of underground passages throughout this desert that date back more than a thousand years. They've been added to through the ages. It could take days, perhaps weeks, to find her. If ever."

Michael turned to one of the agents from Kabul. "Do what you have to do, but get me as many men as you can here by daybreak."

When they were alone again, Khalid pointed to Rahab, who mercifully someone had covered with a blanket. "Who was this woman that someone would want her dead? She played some part. She knew something. Important enough for Laura to risk her life to find out. She had information about your missing agent.

You know her, don't you?"

Michael didn't look at Khalid, but he knew the tribesman had seen the truth. It was time to do some damage control. "No, I don't know her." That much was true. He hadn't spoken to her in years. The last he'd seen her he barely recognized her. This time was no different. Their time apart hadn't been kind to Rahab and she was *Booth's* contact.

He trusted her. Michael did not. "How do you know the person missing is an agent of my government?"

Nothing showed in Khalid's blank expression. "The time for playing games is over, my friend. You need my help. And I want to know what I'm getting myself and my people involved in."

Michael took his time answering. To confide in someone outside of the Agency was as close to treason as it got. Booth had confided in Rahab and look where that had gotten him. But was keeping the Agency's secrets worth any more loss of life? He was almost certain Rachel had little time left before she, too, became another victim of this secret war. He feared he'd lost his best friend to it already.

Michael stepped away from the other agents and motioned for Khalid to follow. Resentment trailed in the wake of each of Khalid's steps.

"All right. I'll tell you what I believe you need to know. You're right. The man missing is one of ours."

"You are CIA."

Michael wasn't surprised Khalid had figured it out. But what did it say about the state of Khalid's world if someone like this tribesman was familiar with the workings of another country's spy network?

"Yes. The man missing was sent here to find Zyad Ali-Arawar."

Khalid recognized the name. "The man is a ghost. Your government is looking for someone as elusive as the former Bin Laden himself was."

Michael forced a smile. "Perhaps. Agent Tanner had orders to capture Zyad Ali-Arawar alive, if possible. We believed that bringing this man in secretly, without the fanfare of the press, would lead us to more of the top al-Qaeda leaders."

"Your government has been trying to destroy al-Qaeda for years. What makes you think you can do so now?"

"We had intel that Zyad Ali-Arawar was in this area."

"Why not send in your marines to surround the area? Ensure that the man didn't escape."

Michael's lack of answer confirmed Khalid suspicions. "I see. There is more to the story than simply wanting to capture Ali-Arawar, isn't there?"

Khalid was correct. There was more to the story. Much more.

Chapter Six

The man with the knife slapped my face hard with a closed fist. The blow forced my head back and sideways.

He was wearing something, a ring, and brass knuckles. I could feel welts rising on my cheek. He was well trained. Working the intimidation factor. He then spoke to me in Arabic, trying to determine how much I might have understood.

It took all of my past training to keep a blank expression. Again he fired off question after question in Arabic.

I shook my head. "I don't understand."

"You lie." He'd switched to English since he wasn't completely convinced I knew the language.

"I don't know what you mean. Why have you brought me here?"

He slapped me again, this time harder. "Enough. Stop lying. I know why you are here. You've come to find the agent. Booth Tanner. I had the pleasure of ending his life."

Please, God, no.

I struggled to keep my reaction to those gut-wrenching words from showing. Unfortunately, my assailant had seen the truth. He smiled slowly. "It's true. His death came slow. He suffered much," he continued as if enjoying the story. "Yours does not have to be painful. I can make it swift. If you cooperate."

I refused to take his bait. "Like Rahab? I saw what you did to her. She'd been tortured before you killed her."

The man who had been little more than a voice attached to the knife moved closer, inches from my face. For the first time, I was able to make out some of his features.

He was Arabic, which, of course, was no great surprise, considering his dialect. He leered at me then said something I didn't understand to the others and they laughed once more. I tried to discern their numbers from the sound of their laughter. Two, possibly three, men.

My assailant whispered against my ear, his hot, foul breath fanning across my cheek. "She deserved everything she got. She was one of us. She became a traitor for your man. She sold herself and her country out for money."

I didn't believe for a minute that Rahab was al-Qaeda but paying an operative was commonplace. I'd seen the conditions of Rahab's life. It wouldn't have been easy to choose to help Booth. If what this man said was true, why had Rahab chosen to try and reach out to me after Booth disappeared? No amount of money could have forced her to risk her life and her family's to help a stranger.

The Arab grabbed a handful of my hair and yanked me closer. "You will tell me what you know. And you will do it now." His tone grew hard. He didn't like that I wasn't completely intimidated by him.

The knife's edge slithered across my cheek, slicing into it. I closed my eyes. I didn't want to see excitement in his. "I don't know what you want me to say. I don't know anything."

The knife's tip dug deeper into my cheek. "Liar. You know plenty. Now, I want to know what you know about the weapons. What did Tanner tell you?"

What you know about the weapons?

My thoughts tangled. Why would this man whom I'd pegged to be al-Qaeda believe Booth or I would know something about weapons?

"What weapons? I don't know anything about any weapons."

Somewhere a phone rang. The man questioning me removed the knife and gripped my face painfully in his hand.

I could feel the blood from my cuts oozing down my face.

"Hussein." One of the men behind him interrupted his questioning. "He wants to speak with you."

My assailant, Hussein, expelled a harsh breath. He hadn't liked that his cohort had used his name, which meant it was his real name and not an alias. He squeezed my face harder, then released me, and stormed away.

The relief washing over me threatened consciousness. I strained to grasp bits of the conversation. The man who'd identified Hussein whispered something that sounded like, 'he's angry', then Hussein took the phone and moved away.

The conversation was almost completely unintelligible except for a couple of words. Hussein slammed the phone shut and said something to the men about covering tracks. With that and only a glance my way, they left the bunker, relocking the door.

In Hussein's conversation with what I could only conclude was the real mastermind responsible for my kidnapping, I'd caught the words CIA and search. Someone from my former team was looking for me. Had Khalid gotten word to them? I could only pray they'd find me before Hussein finished the job.

* * * *

"Michael, I have someone who claims to have seen Rahab before she died. He said he followed her outside of the village." Dawn had barely broken when the search for Rachel resumed.

Sam found him going over the map provided by Khalid. As Michael soon discovered, the tribesmen of the desert possessed a great deal of modern tools.

Michael studied Khalid's expression at this piece of news. In the short length of time he'd known the tribesman, he'd learned the man rarely gave anything he was feeling away. No doubt, a trait that came in handy in this section of the world. Here you never knew whom to trust.

Michael glanced past Sam to the Arab standing nearby. "How did this guy find out about the search? Did he see something? Maybe he knows who killed Rahab and took Laura?" At this point, everyone was questionable. But with few leads and thousands of miles of desert to search, no clue could be ignored.

"He is from the village of Bel-Ahzar. He saw...Laura and Khalid the other day. It aroused his suspicions about Rahab, who he knows. He might be of some help."

Michael looked the man over. He didn't stand out as unusual but then, at this point, the enemy could be disguised as anyone. "What's his name?"

"Mozhar."

Michael turned to Khalid. "Do you know him?"

"I've seen him around the village. I believe he sometimes brings perishables in from Kabul and gives candy to the children."

Michael turned back to the man. He motioned to Mozhar, who was standing out of earshot. "Do you speak English?" The man nodded. "You know something?"

"Yes. As I explained to your friend, I knew Rahab and her family. Well, what's left of her family. There's just her mother now. The bombs struck the village a few years back and destroyed most of it."

Michael glanced at Khalid, who nodded. "How did you find out about the search?"

"I travel this route several times a month. I arrived in Bel-Ahzar only yesterday. As I was on my way late in the evening, I saw Rahab leaving the village. She was alone."

"And you followed her?"

"No, no, I was traveling west to Ala-Ahaia. I confess I thought it strange she would be leaving the village that late, but I was in a hurry. I had vegetables for Ala-Ahaia that needed to be there before sundown."

"Did you see anyone follow her out of the village?"

Michael had a feeling he knew the answer. Whoever had killed Rahab and taken Rachel was a pro. They knew what they were doing and how to hide in plain sight.

"No, I'm sorry, I did not. But I wish now that I'd listened to my conscience and followed Rahab. She might still be alive."

As Michael was quickly learning in his crash course of fieldwork, you couldn't always trust the enemy to look the part. Still, the man appeared harmless enough and according to Khalid, his story checked out. "We can use all the help we can get. Why don't you go with Sam? He can get you started."

Sam motioned to Mozhar. "Sure, come with me. You can work with me."

Once the Arab was out of sight, Michael asked Khalid, "Where do you think they'd be keeping her?"

Khalid shrugged. "There are several places that come to mind. No doubt, they'll move her around a lot, especially once they hear of the search."

Michael had no doubt that whoever took Rachel would be watching the area carefully. They'd expect someone to come looking for her.

"Give me your best guess." Michael had never felt

more frustrated. His time for bringing Rachel back had run out long ago and yet he'd ignored Hughes' calls. Which probably meant Hughes would be adding his name to the growing list of problems to take care of.

Khalid moved back to the map spread out on a makeshift table. "If it were me, I'd take her here." He jabbed a finger on a site called Ulziheir. The last known hideout of some of the top al-Qaeda leaders. The sickening feeling in the pit of Michael's stomach increased tenfold.

That entire area had been impenetrable since the invasion of Afghanistan. The last stronghold of both Taliban fugitives and al-Qaeda operatives that U.S. troops hadn't been able to destroy. It was also a suspected training camp for al-Qaeda.

"That's not what I needed to hear." If Rachel had been taken there, the chances of her coming out of this thing alive were next to zero. And he'd have a hard time explaining to the world how he'd gotten an American under-ambassador murdered in enemy territory.

* * * *

Blinding light filled the room. It took forever for my eyes to adjust to the brilliance. Then, the world returned to darkness. I'd gotten only a glimpse around me. The walls were gray, reinforced cement blocks. No windows, and bags holding what appeared to be some type of grain were stacked high against one wall. Beyond that, nothing but blinding desert sun.

I'd caught sight of two men entering the room. Once

the door slammed shut, they talked quietly. I couldn't make out much of their conversation--only that they needed to wait for Hussein before moving me.

I had a feeling if I left this place, I'd be leaving behind my last chance at getting out of this alive.

One of the two came close. I could smell sweat and stale food--a combination of garlic and something else-- on his breath. He put something to my lips. A bottle of water. My captors were showing compassion. They needed me alive. For the first time since I'd awakened to this nightmare, I let myself hope. There might be a chance I could survive if help came soon.

The water was good and did wonders to bring me back to life. I remembered something Booth had taught me once.

He'd told me that when captured, I should try and make my assailants see me as a human being. It became harder to kill someone who you'd made a connection with.

"Why are you doing this? I know nothing." The man with the water froze then turned back to me. I couldn't tell if he'd understood what I'd said and I didn't dare address him in Arabic. "My name is Laura. Laura Ingalls. I'm from Texas. Do you know where that is?"

The man disappeared into the darkness. He said something quietly to his buddy.

"I have a two-year-old daughter. I'm all that she has. If you kill me, you'll destroy her."

"Shut up," one of the men told me in broken English. "You will shut up now."

"Her name is Ava. Do you have children of your

own?"

After one of them rattled off profanity in Arabic, they left the bunker. I could hear them speaking angrily to each other outside. I slumped against the ropes holding my hands, more desperate than ever.

If I didn't find a way to escape soon, I'd be killed once they got what they wanted out of me.

I somehow managed to find the strength to stand on my tiptoes, which relieved the tension on the ropes a fraction. The knot was simple enough, but it would be all but impossible to work loose from the position my hands were tied. The tiniest amount of light filtered through the cement blocks above. There were wood beam supports to which my ropes had been attached. Something above my hands glinted in faint light. It took me a second or two to realize it was a wood screw. It had worked its way halfway out of its hole. Probably due to my weight against the beam. I stretched my fingers out as far as I could and managed to touch the screw. It hurt like crazy, but I began to work it from its place, being extremely careful not to drop it.

After half a dozen useless attempts, I somehow managed to get the screw loose and clasped it between my thumb and forefinger.

If I could move a little more to my right and stand a little higher on my tiptoes, I could position the screw against the knot in the rope and hopefully get it loose.

I got the screw positioned and slowly began to work the knot while listening for any sound outside. The men were silent. I didn't know if they'd left or simply decided to keep quiet.

I worked for what seemed like hours and had managed to loosen the knot slightly when I heard voices again from outside. I recognized Hussein's immediately. I tucked the screw into the palm of my hand and prayed it wouldn't be discovered.

The door swung back hard on its hinges to admit Hussein, followed by his two subordinates.

Hussein ordered the two men to clear the place. Make it as if no one had been there. Leave no evidence behind. Then he came to me, his expression cold and hard. The face of a killer. Before I knew what he was intending to do, he raised his right hand and jabbed something into my neck, then darkness slowly began to swallow me. I fought to hang on to consciousness, but it was as if I were walking through a thick fog. I couldn't keep my eyes open.

My hands were released and I struggled to keep the screw hidden. I heard Hussein tell one of the men to get me inside the Jeep and under the tarp.

"No," I managed to whisper, yet no one was listening. Not that it mattered. I was powerless to do anything more but slump into the arms of my captor. Before there was nothing at all, I prayed that Ava would never hear the details of what happened to me.

Chapter Seven

I was startled awake from sweet dreams of Ava when someone's open hand made contact with my cheek. The smacking sound of flesh on flesh reverberated throughout my body. Slowly, I opened my eyes and looked into Hussein's.

He eyed me suspiciously for a handful of seconds. Satisfied I was now fully awake, he turned away. He addressed someone in Arabic. "She's awake."

"Good." The voice, a new player, sounded oddly familiar. I glanced around. I was huddled in the corner of a room only slightly more endearing than the last one. At least my hands weren't tied above my head. Now they were secured behind my back. I still clutched the screw tight in my palm. Somehow, against all odds, I'd managed to hold on to it.

The familiar voice stepped from the shadows. It was Anwar. The man who'd provided me safe passage to

Kabul.

Disbelief kept me from speaking for a moment. My mind raced to make logical sense of what I was seeing.

"Anwar? What are you doing?"

He ignored my question. "You will tell me what you know about the weapons and you will do it now."

This was not the man who'd appeared caring. David's trusted friend.

"What weapons? I don't know anything about any weapons. I told you why I was here."

He squinted furiously at me. When he spoke, each of the words were bitten out, angry spittle flying from his mouth. "You are lying. If you're trying to protect him, you're wasting your breath. If you want to save yourself and your daughter, you will do as I suggest and tell me what you know. Everything."

"My daughter? What are you talking about?" I struggled to force those words out, my thoughts reeling from the implication. He knew about Ava. How? I'd mentioned my daughter to the two men, but I had a feeling Anwar's admission had nothing to do with them. This man knew David. He'd ingratiated himself into David's life with a specific purpose. To get to me.

"That's right. You figured it out. I know all about you and I can get to your daughter any time I choose. You will answer my question."

I fought back bile. "I don't know anything about any weapons. As I told you, I came to find my friend. Nothing more. That's it."

Anwar motioned to one of the men, who yanked me to my feet and ripped my shirt open in the back.

Hussein stepped forward carrying a whip, a maniacal grin on his face. He motioned for the man to turn me around.

The first blow from the whip knocked me to my knees along with the man who held me.

"Get her to her feet," Anwar bellowed. The man lifted me up. The second blow struck my lower back. I struggled to keep conscious as blow after blow rained down on my back. I lost track of their numbers before Hussein was finally told to stop.

The man released me and I fell forward to the floor, slipping in and out of consciousness.

Anwar discussed what must be done next. "He will not be pleased. The chance that she may have told someone about this is risky, but if we cannot break her, then it will have to do." Though I pretended to be unconscious, Anwar didn't seem worried. Which meant they didn't plan on letting me walk out of this place alive.

Somehow, in spite of the merciless beating, I'd held onto the screw as if holding onto my only means of escape.

"Do you want me to kill her?" Hussein seemed excited by the possibility.

"Not yet. I must speak with him first. See how far he wants us to take this thing."

"What do we do with her?" Hussein kicked my side, checking to see if I was awake.

"Her? She's not going anywhere. You and your men keep guard on her. I will need to talk to him in person. We cannot risk someone intercepting the call. Her people are everywhere. Lucky for us, they will not look here. Still, it's too much of a risk."

"Do you want me to keep trying to break her?" Hussein asked.

Anwar hesitated for a moment, considering my torture as if making a business decision. "No. If you were going to break her, that beating would have done it. We'll have to try something different. There's the child. That's something to consider, but first I must talk to him."

Hussein seemed disappointed. "All right, but if her people come here, we will have no choice but to kill her."

Anwar opened the door, letting in blinding sunlight before he turned around to face Hussein. "You will do as you are told and nothing more. If you cannot follow commands, I will have to find someone else to replace you. Zyad Ali-Arawar will not be pleased. And if Zyad isn't happy, heads are going to roll."

If Zyad isn't happy. Anwar was working for al-Qaeda second in command. How had the seemingly innocent Anwar come to report to one of the top ten terrorists in the world?

Then another realization hit. Did this have something to do with the upcoming Israeli-Palestine talks involving the Secretary of State? Was Zyad planning an attack when many of the key Middle East leaders were in one place along with U.S. Diplomats? Was that the plan all along? Had Booth discovered Zyad's scheme and had it cost him his life as Anwar had suggested? I hoped not.

Hussein ordered one of the two men with him to get

me up. The man, the one who'd given me water, jerked me into a sitting position. My back hit the wall hard and I cried out. The pain was excruciating.

"Give her something to drink. I have to go out for a while. If he calls, tell him I stepped out for a smoke, understood?" Hussein eyed the man menacingly for a second longer, then left.

It took all my willpower to shove my wounded body away from the wall an inch. I glanced at the two men guarding me, but they seemed disinterested. In spite of the fact that any little movement brought my injured back closer to the wall, I had to try to free myself from the ropes. I managed to position the screw right to work it back and forth against the rope while keeping a close eye on the men. In this light, they appeared little more than boys. New recruits in the war of terror still raging in spite of the U.S's efforts otherwise.

Outside, a Jeep fired to life, its tired old engine growing fainter in the distance. One of the two, the same young man who brought me water, came and inspected my wounds.

The expression on his face said enough to confirm what I suspected. It was bad. He tried to ease the tattered pieces of my shirt back into place.

The other young man dug out a pack of cigarettes and offered one to his friend. They stepped outside, leaving me alone with my thoughts.

I leaned my head against my knees and continued to work on the rope.

None of what I'd learned made any sense. I tried to replay the facts, as I knew them in my head. I had to believe this whole thing had been set into motion because Booth had unwillingly uncovered something big. Had he tried to get word to me before his death and somehow entrusted Rahab, his operative, with the truth? After Booth disappeared, Rahab kept trying to warn me of something.

If that were true, then I was back to square one. And this thing had nothing to do with Booth or me. We were victims by association.

This was bigger than the two of us. And as old as the battle that raged between Arab and Jew.

* * * *

"There's evidence someone has been here recently." One of the agents stationed in Kandahar knelt and examined the floor at a certain spot. Though it was barely midday, the underground bunker was pitch dark inside. Someone connected a flood light that filled the twenty by twenty space with light.

Agent Sheridan studied something on the dirt floor.

Michael knelt next to him. Half a dozen dark blotches the size of pennies covered the floor. "Is that?"

"Blood," Agent Sheridan confirmed. His gaze went to the ceiling and Michael's followed. "Someone was tied here. See the rub marks left from the rope?"

Michael did. "How long ago? Is there any way of telling?"

Khalid knelt next to them and dabbed his finger onto one of the dark dots. He rubbed it between his thumb and finger. "I'd say the blood is only a few days old."

"Do you think she's still alive?" Michael directed the question to the one person he sort of trusted.

Khalid's gaze fell on him. "Maybe when she left here. There's not all that much blood. Not enough to be the result of a fatal injury."

Michael got to his feet. "Do you still believe they would take her to Ulziheir?"

"If they are al-Qaeda, then yes. It makes the most sense. They'd be safest there," Khalid told him.

Michael tried to think. What would Booth do in this situation? The answer came to him as clear as if Booth had spoken it. Go after her. Bring her back if possible. No matter if it cost him his life.

"Can you get me in there?"

Khalid's stony expression gave nothing away. "Do you have any idea what you are asking? The danger?"

"I'm not asking you to come with me. I need to find a way in. Tell me where you think they'd hold her. That's all I'm asking."

After a moment, Khalid agreed. "I'll help you only if I *can* come along. In good conscience, I cannot send you out there alone. You would not survive."

"Thank you, but this is no longer your problem. I'll bring Sam and the two agents with me."

Michael moved to pass him, but Khalid blocked him with his body. "Let me ask you this, do you trust them?"

Trust. The only person he trusted beyond himself and Booth was Sam. Slowly, he shook his head. "Not entirely. I don't know the two men with us. Sam, I'd trust with my life."

"Then he is the only one we will take. And if you

want to bring her back alive, you will not let the other two know where we are going."

* * * *

"Have you found anything?" Director Hughes' stress level continued to grow with Agent Michael Bernard's silence.

He'd told Bernard he had twenty-four hours to bring her in. That was two days ago. While he knew Booth and Bernard were close, it wouldn't be the first time a friend had betrayed another friend. When it came to money and the threat of losing your life, stronger friendships than theirs had failed.

When his calls to Bernard continued to go unanswered, he turned to another source.

"No, sir. Nothing yet. We know he arrived in Kabul. He met with the two agents we assigned to him. Sheridan and Jones, I trust implicitly. But something's definitely going on there. I can't reach Sheridan or Jones on their secure lines and Sam's radio is silent."

Hughes swallowed back his misgivings and let loose a string of four letter words. He should have listened to his wife and retired two years ago, after the first heart attack. If he got through this thing without going to prison, he could almost guarantee a second attack.

He took a deep breath, rubbing a sweaty hand over his disappearing hairline. "Any word on Booth or the woman?"

"Nothing, sir."

"What about *him*? Does he suspect anything?"

"Not yet. Not as far as I can tell. I think he's getting nervous, though. Which means the situation has become grave."

And it kept getting better and better. Hughes propelled his girth from the leather chair and walked over to the office window that reflected back the lateness of the day.

The sun had set on D.C. hours earlier. "I need you on the ground. How soon can you get there?"

"I'm on my way now."

"Will he suspect?"

"He's distracted. There's a lot going on right now. I can make it happen. I'll fake an illness."

"Good. Get there. Get her out of there--if she's still alive. What about the others?"

"I have someone watching them."

One ray of light on this otherwise dark day in the trenches. "Good. Good. I'm counting on you. Do what you have to do, but get her out of there."

* * * *

"We are set, then?" Khalid glanced from Michael to Sam, who had lost their Western clothing and were now dressed in traditional Arab attire. He waited until both men were astride their horses. They looked out of place there as well.

Khalid kicked the mount into motion, tossing them a final word of warning over his shoulder. "From here on out you will do as I say."

His nephew would travel with them. He trusted

Alain with his life. He hated that he was putting the young man's life in jeopardy, but he could not--would not--let the woman die in such a manner. He'd believed her. Her only purpose here was to find the man who was her child's father and bring him home if at all possible. He admired such loyalty. The others were there for political gain, money, or worse. Some false sense of patriotism.

Khalid glanced over his shoulder at the two men awkwardly reining their mounts. He didn't know what to make of them yet. His gut told him they wanted to bring the woman home and the agent if possible, but he still didn't know where their loyalties lay.

"Do you think they have Laura's best interest at heart?" Alain whispered once they were a good way ahead, reading his thoughts.

"I don't know. Something more is going on here than what we are being told. Are you ready to deal with it if this thing blows up in our faces?"

"Of course. Whatever you need me to do. You know that."

"Yes, you are always trustworthy, Alain. My sister would be proud."

Alain was pleased by his compliment. He'd idolized his uncle since he was a young boy. "Do you think we'll find Laura alive?"

"If we don't find her soon, she won't be. I can only imagine the things she's had to endure. If she is alive, she won't be the same when she comes out of it."

"And this Agent Booth?"

"I think we will find him dead. It's been too long.

Too much time has passed. You know al-Qaeda's tactics. They have no mercy and they don't believe in leaving witnesses behind."

* * * *

Was it my imagination or did the knot loosen a bit? I tugged at my wrists. There was definitely more play between them. I glanced up at my two captors. They'd been busy playing cards for a while now. Hussein hadn't returned.

But I didn't trust him not to go against Anwar's command and take matters into his own hands. I started working the knot with more vengeance than ever. The two men appeared armed only with knives. If I could get my hands free, I might be able to lure one of them over and overpower him, get the knife from him before his partner could come to his aid.

I was willing to bet the two would have some form of transportation. I worked the screw deeper into the knot. I'd been at it for hours. Once, the young man who'd given me water tried to put something on my wounds. I'd refused, pretending to be in pain. I was afraid he'd seen the ropes loosened if I allowed him to get close. Not that it took a whole lot of effort to fake the pain. The slightest movement of working the screw was nearly unbearable.

It took less than half an hour more for the knot to loosen enough for me to slip my left hand out. I worked the rope free of my right hand and wiggled my fingers. They were stiff from the work effort.

I knew my time was quickly running out. I needed to act now before Hussein returned.

I shifted into a better position that would allow me to spring to my feet quickly. Then, I moaned. The two men glanced at me then at each other. One grabbed a bottle of water close by and came over to where I sat.

He held the water to my lips. The knife was inches from me. His partner had taken the opportunity to look at his cards. I took another sip of water before lunging for the knife. I was on my feet before he knew what I was doing. I slit his throat in a single fluid motion. He fell away from me, dead. The second man jumped to his feet and snatched his knife from the table.

He charged toward me. I dodged his attempts easily enough then plunged the knife deep into his back. He careened forward, landing on top of his partner. I knelt next to them and felt for a pulse. I knew they were dead. I needed assurances. My first instinct was to rush outside to freedom. I forced myself to take a moment to listen. I heard nothing but the unnerving silence of the desert. I took the knife from the last man I'd killed then searched both of their pockets. They were carrying cell phones and a little money. The first man I'd killed had a gun.

I took it along with both phones and the money. Slowly, I advanced to the door and opened it a crack, listening for any out of place sound. I'd lost all track of time. It was dark outside. The night sky was filled with thousands of stars.

To the back of the bunker was a beat up Jeep. The keys were in the ignition. It took several cranks for the worn out engine to turn over. I put the vehicle in gear and headed away from the bunker without turning on any lights. When I was a safe distance away, I parked the Jeep and tried to find a map to tell me where I was. The Jeep appeared to be full of fuel. The few meager possessions I'd brought with me had been tossed into the back floorboard. The prepaid phone was missing. The cell phone I used back home was there. I dug it out, then reconsidered using it. I might be leading whoever was responsible for my capture beyond Anwar and Hussein straight to me if they were monitoring the phone.

Inside the glove box, I found something resembling energy bars, which I tossed on the seat next to me, and a folded, well-worn map. Without knowing where I was at this point, I had no idea how to figure out where I was going on the map, which meant I'd have to rely on gut instinct.

I guessed my captors would have taken me into enemy territory. Which meant to get to safer ground, I'd need to head south.

I put the Jeep in gear again, still traveling without lights and headed due south.

After I'd driven a good click without seeing anything but open desert, I wondered what lay out there in the dark beyond the occasional animal scurrying to safety.

I hadn't eaten in days. The lack of food left me weak and struggling to stay focused. The energy bars weren't exactly appealing, but I wasn't in a position to be picky.

I ate the bar with relish and reached for another when one of the men's cell phones rang. I wasn't sure why I'd taken their phones except that in the off chance I escaped, something on them might hold a lead to Booth.

I was beginning to wonder the wisdom of my actions when a few minutes later, the second cell phone rang.

How long would it be before Hussein and Anwar came after me? Not long, especially when the two men didn't answer their phones.

The desert was filled with miles and miles of darkness, which left plenty of time for my thoughts to wander. It didn't take long before Ava's face appeared before me. What would she be thinking right now? Did she miss me? Was she worried? The thought of her made me want to reach out to her. Hear her voice. I didn't dare risk making that call. Not yet. But, the idea of her worrying made my heart sick. I couldn't think about what she'd go through if I didn't return and not go crazy. The image of my precious daughter standing over my grave infuriated me and gave me the incentive to survive this thing for her.

I continued to make my way south until daybreak. I hadn't come across another human being in hours, no nomads, no makeshift villages. Not another human life.

Nothing but desert. That in itself was enough to prick my cop's intuition.

If I kept on this course, would I travel straight into enemy territory? I needed help. I didn't know whom to believe and I wasn't convinced that Michael hadn't set me up. There was only one person I knew I could trust. David. I needed to warn him about Anwar. I prayed that by reaching out to him I wouldn't be leading the trouble following me straight to his door.

Out of sheer desperation, I grabbed my phone. The familiar sound of his fatherly voice was such a relief that

I started to cry. "David, it's me."

"Oh, Rachel. Are you okay? I've been worried sick about you. I've been trying to reach you."

I bit back a shaky sob. "Yes, I'm fine. I'm sorry. David, I don't know how secure this phone is. Anwar isn't your friend. I was kidnapped by him."

"Kidnapped." The fear in his tone was easy to read.

"It's okay. I'm fine, I managed to escape."

"My goodness, Rachel. I can't believe it. But why? Did he hurt you?"

"No, I'm okay. And I'm not sure what's going on. None of this makes any sense. I thought when Booth went missing, he was the key. Now, I'm not sure. Maybe they were after me all along. Maybe that's why Anwar got close to you. To bring about this opportunity. He kept asking me what I knew about the weapons."

"Weapons? What weapons could he be talking about? Do you think this has anything to do with the peace talks?"

"I have no idea, but the timing is a pretty huge coincidence, don't you think?" I took a deep breath and told him everything. "David, I had to kill two people. I'm in the middle of the desert and I don't know where I am. I need your help. I know it's asking a lot and you wanted to keep the embassy out of this, but I need your help."

"Of course, Rachel, whatever you need. Rest assured, I'm going to move heaven and earth to get you out of there. Tell me everything you know. Let's retrace your steps. Maybe we can figure it out from there."

For the first time since I'd awakened to the reality of

being kidnapped, I allowed myself this small glimmer of hope. *Thank You, God.*

"We need to keep this brief. There's not much time." I quickly told him the details of my terrifying capture and the sickening feeling of having taken two lives that had plummeted me back into the world I'd thought I'd left behind for good.

"I went out into the desert near Bel-Ahzar to meet someone who told me she had news about Booth, but when I got there, she'd been murdered. Someone ambushed me from behind and knocked me out."

"What happened after that?"

"That's just it. I don't know. David, I was moved. My gut tells me the first place was close to where I was taken. It was some sort of cement bunker. The second location appeared to be in the middle of nowhere. I managed to get away by killing the two men watching me. And I don't know where I am."

"Did they say anything that might help you identify who they worked for?"

"No. There was a third man, someone named Hussein, and Anwar kept mentioning he needed to speak to someone else. I took it to mean the person in charge." I hesitated for a moment. "David, Hussein mentioned Zyad Ali-Arawar."

"The al-Qaeda's second in command?"

"Yes. I know. This thing is big. We need to get in touch with someone at the CIA. Agent Melinda James is a good place to start and I trust her. Whatever you do, don't talk to Director Hughes and make sure Melinda doesn't either. I *don't* trust him."

"Your former boss?" David was clearly shocked.

"Yes, he's involved in this somehow."

"I will call Ms. James right away. And you're right. This thing has the potential for international repercussions. Especially if it gets out that our people might have known about it beforehand. But how do we get you out of there and to safety? Is there someplace you can go? Someplace safe?"

"I don't know. I'm in the middle of the desert. I haven't seen anything resembling a village or house since I left the bunker."

"I see. That will present a problem."

"David, I'm running out of time. I'm a sitting duck here. I don't know where I am. I need you to have Melinda trace this phone's location."

"They can do that?" He seemed surprised.

"Yes. They have satellites that can track its exact location. I'll leave it on for a while and continue driving."

"Okay, Rachel. I'll get started on it right away. We'll get you out of this. But please be careful. Don't take any unnecessary risks. Rachel, you should know there are people on the ground searching for you. Please be careful."

Michael had agents looking for me. They wouldn't fail at their mission. They couldn't. Too much was at stake. "I will. David, is Ava okay?"

"Of course, my dear, she's fine. She misses her mommy, though."

I shoved back raw, strangling emotions always present when I thought about my daughter and the things

I'd risked by coming here. Had I risked my life and my daughter's happiness in vain? Booth might have already been dead before I arrived. The chance of that being the truth was growing with each new realization.

"Listen, David, if something should happen to me, if I don't get out of this thing alive, please promise me you'll take care of Ava for me."

"Rachel, don't talk like that. Don't even think it. You're going to be fine. I'll make sure of it."

I held onto that promise with all my heart. "Hurry, David. I don't want my daughter to have to bury both her parents to this cause."

Chapter Eight

Hughes recognized the number right away. "Yes?"

"I'm on the ground."

"Excellent. I expected nothing less. Tell me what's happening there."

"There's a massive search underway. Michael has called out all the stops in spearheading a major deployment of agents to the area."

"Michael? You've spoken to him?"

"No. I thought it best not to give away my cover."

"Yes, that's wise. Do you know anything yet?"

"I've managed to reach my contact and have spoken to him in depth." Hughes' silence following the man's revelation was clearly anticipated. "Don't worry, I trust him explicitly. He tells me the search is primarily to find Rachel. The feeling here is that Agent Tanner is dead already. There's no effort, at least not visible, being made to find him."

Hughes blew out a breath. This thing might still be contained yet. "I think that's for the best right now, don't you? Let's try and keep it that way."

"Yes, I agree. I'll handle it."

Hughes glanced out his window as the first pale-pink light split the eastern sky. "Do you have any idea what's happened to her?"

The lengthy pause was foreboding. His answer, when it came, was less reassuring. "It doesn't look good, I'm afraid. Obviously, Rahab knew something worth dying for. I think she was trying to get word to Rachel. Perhaps she knew the real mission behind the ruse."

"Did she take it to her grave?" Hughes wasn't sure which to hope for.

"I'd say the probability of that is great. My contact tells me she was tortured. But sir, with all due respect, whether or not Rahab gave information to her killers doesn't matter. My contact tells me Rachel was scheduled to meet Rahab. The chances are Rahab was tortured into giving that up. They were expecting Rachel. She didn't stand a chance."

Hughes let out a frustrated sigh. This thing was quickly escaping his control. "Does your man have any idea where they might be holding her? I don't need to tell you we need to get her out of there alive, before Michael and his team reach her. When this thing explodes, the last thing we need on our hands is another death."

It was now no longer a matter of if it reached the eyes of the world, but when.

"My guy knows the desert like the back of his hand.

He'll know where to find her if anyone can."

Hughes heard the reservations in the man's voice. "But."

"But he's concerned for her wellbeing. He's been helping with the search. They're already in enemy territory."

"Then how will you get to him without the others finding out?"

The confidence in his agent's voice reminded Hughes why he'd chosen him for this mission. "I know the way. I'll reach him by sunset. We've organized a meeting place. He will update me on Michael's progress. Not all is lost. I'll be able to keep track of the others this way. If they're the ones responsible for this, then they'll not want her to be brought back alive."

"Yes. Yes, that's a good idea. Well done."

"Thank you. I should go. It's doubtful anyone is listening in, but the less time we spend speaking, the less likely someone can connect us to each other."

Hughes had to agree. The last thing he needed was someone from the enemy camp to get wind of his man on the ground. "Yes. You'll let me know the moment you have word?"

"Of course. Hopefully the next time we speak I'll have good news."

* * * *

"There's a small outpost west of Ulziheir. It was once a watch post for al-Qaeda's training camp. From there, a person can see anyone coming for miles away.

It's dangerous. We could be walking into an ambush. But I'm betting this is where they've taken her," Khalid assured him.

Michael considered the possibility. "Then how can we get in there without being spotted?"

"Chances are we won't. We'll wait until dark and advance as quietly as possible. We can only hope for some element of surprise."

Michael glanced at his watch. Darkness wouldn't come for another three-plus hours. Ulziheir was some fifty kilometers away.

"What do we do in the meantime?"

Khalid observed him curiously. He'd seen that look many times today. "Do? We'll need to rest. It will be a long night. A dangerous night, for sure. We will need all of our wits to get through this night alive."

Michael wondered for half a second if Khalid might possibly be joking. The expression on the tribesman's face had never been more serious.

Khalid answered the question he hadn't asked. "I do not kid about such things. If you do not rest, you will be useless to us." Khalid pointed to where the horses had been tied. "You will find a mat in your animal's pack. Those trees near the rocks will allow sufficient release from the sun. Rest, my friend. Otherwise, I will be forced to leave you behind."

* * * *

"I do not have much time before they become suspicious." His contact glanced over his shoulder. The meet, taking place at exactly sunset, appeared to have gone off smoothly enough. Which spooked him. He'd long ago learned nothing went this smoothly. The abandoned house south of an outcropping of trees provided enough privacy to keep anyone passing by from spotting the two men.

"I understand. I'll be brief. What do you know?"

"Nothing more than what I've told you. The search is for the woman. We believe she is being held at the outpost near Ulziheir. There's a raid scheduled for tonight."

He hesitated. How much should he divulge to his contact? Where did his true loyalties lie? If he kept quiet, would he be sending this man to his grave along with Agent Bernard as well as the rest of his team? "She won't be there. She's escaped."

His contact studied him. "I see. And how do you know this?"

"You don't need to know that. You do need to know that you'll find two men dead there." He pulled out the map he carried with him and spread it out on a rock. There wasn't much light left in the day. Hopefully, it would be enough.

"She managed to overpower her captives and get away. I need you to tell me where she might have gone on this map."

His operative ignored his command. That he was angry was evident in the way he spat out the words. "If she's not there, then why waste our time?"

"I need a diversion and at this point there's only one person I trust. I'm sorry, my friend, but it isn't you."

His informant forced a smile. "That's good because I don't trust you, either."

Honesty among spies. That made him laugh. "Then we're even. Also, there may be people working with you now who are not what they seem. Be careful, my friend."

"Always. Since there is no immediate danger waiting for me, do you wish me to delay the raid until morning?"

"No, absolutely not. It would only call suspicion to your motives. Keep to the schedule." He leaned over the map and squinted. There wasn't much daylight left. Time was running out. "She was heading south from the last report. Tell me where she might be."

His contact searched the map then jabbed a finger to a small outcropping of rocks in the middle of desert. "If it was me, and I was running for my life, I'd hide out there during the day and move only at night. Which means, she'll be on the move soon."

"Yes, and that's one hundred kilometers at least."

"Exactly. I'd suggest you move forward without your lights at a slow speed to keep from drawing any undue attention. You're in enemy territory now. If you're caught, there will be no one to come to your aid."

He straightened and shook his contact's hand. "I will. The moment I have her and we're back in safer territory I'll be in touch. In the meantime, watch your back. You don't know who to trust."

* * * *

With the last rays of sun all but gone, the

temperature in the desert became almost bearable once more. I'd tried to sleep but managed only a minute here and there in the shadow of the rock where I tried to keep the Jeep hidden from anyone who might be searching the area.

I dared not call David again. I couldn't risk someone tracking my movements by phone. I'd turned off the cell I'd given him to trace my whereabouts after the first half hour. No need to push my luck any further. I didn't know what technology al-Qaeda might have at their disposal.

They had the financial support to buy the best. I certainly didn't want to risk being found by them before my team could rescue me.

I'd found something that resembled a first aid kit tucked under a tarp. Armed with the outside mirror and what I assumed was the equivalent of anti-bacterial cream, I did the best I could to treat the wounds left by Hussein's whip and fist. They hurt like crazy and made sleep all but impossible, but they did keep me alert.

I hadn't seen a single living creature in hours. Which was probably a good thing. I was, at my best guess, deep into enemy territory. Anyone venturing my way wouldn't be welcomed.

As the sun lowered in the west, I refueled the Jeep then started the engine. I needed to stay on the move as much as possible. By now, Hussein would have returned to the bunker. He'd know I was on the run.

If my best guess was correct, I had at least another hundred kilometers left to cover before I reached someone who could help, given David's attempts failed to locate me before then. I kept the Jeep's speed at a steady forty clicks an hour to keep the dust at a minimum.

The breeze that reverberated off the desert sand was enough to clear away some of the cobwebs in my head. I'd spent the better part of the day between snatching bits of sleep trying to unravel the mystery that had now become my life.

I had to believe everything was somehow connected to Anwar, perhaps Booth's capture, and no doubt murder. Anwar had ingratiated himself to David with the intent of getting close enough to, at the least, sabotage the peace talks.

At the most, create another 9/11.

What I didn't understand was the weapons part. Hussein and Anwar both had asked me if I knew anything about the weapons. That part of the equation was still a mystery. Could it be that some type of weaponry, possibly some type of suitcase bomb or Weapons of Mass Destruction would be planted at or near the site where the peace talks would take place? Surely, any such plan was destined to fail. The location of the talks was confidential. No one but those granted the highest security knew of it and security would be virtually impossible to penetrate.

By eight, I'd traveled over fifty kilometers and still no sign of any life. I stopped the Jeep and scanned the horizon. Nothing but desert. I turned on my cell phone and saw that David had left a message.

"Rachel, we have an idea where you are. There's a small village some twenty kilometers southwest of you.

I've arranged for two men I trust with my life to meet you there near the center of the town at midnight. One of the men will carry a newspaper. They will take you somewhere secure. Once you're safe, they will call me and I will arrange transportation out of there. Hang in there, my dear. You're almost home. If things go well, you'll be able to tuck Ava in bed tomorrow night."

I closed the phone and leaned against the wheel. I'd tried for a long time to be strong but now with the end in sight I couldn't control my sobs or my tears. I no longer wanted to.

I backtracked and headed the Jeep in the direction David told me to go and prayed that he was right and I'd be with my baby girl soon.

* * * *

"There's no sign of her. The two men have been dead for what I'd guess to be at least twenty-four hours," Sam told him.

Michael shook his head. "The question is, did someone take her or did she escape?"

Khalid's gaze stayed on the two dead men. "She was one of yours. What do you think?"

Michael bent down and picked up something from the dirt floor. The sight of it didn't exactly relieve his uneasiness. "She's out there somewhere. And we're not the only ones looking for her."

Khalid came over to where Michael stood and saw what he held. A cigarette pack bearing an American trademark.

"Those could have been bought off the black market," Khalid told him.

"You don't believe that. Neither do I."

"No. I think we'd better hope we're the first to find out where she is."

Michael could only agree. Both men stepped out into the darkness. "What do we do about those two?" Michael crooked his thumb toward the two dead men.

"Do? We do nothing." Khalid mounted his horse. "We leave them. Let their people take care of them."

Michael shook his head and climbed onto his mount. "Okay, where do we go from here? Where would *she* go?"

Khalid considered the question for a moment. "I'm guessing she'd head south. That's the only logical direction. Unfortunately, there's nothing out there for miles. Your guess is as good as mine. And let's hope she's not seriously injured."

"Where's the nearest village? If she *is* hurt, she'll need attention. Best case, she'll need food."

"There's a small village southwest of here. But I doubt she'd risk going there."

Michael was growing frustrated with dead ends and Khalid's non-responsive answers. "Then where would she go?"

Khalid shrugged. Not exactly comforting. "I don't know. At this point, I think we can't afford to dismiss any possibility. Let's search the village. Who knows, maybe we'll get lucky. If she's not there, then we can only assume she's continued south."

Michael's body ached from the unaccustomed time

spent in the saddle. He'd ridden only a handful of times through the years. It wasn't his thing. But here in the desert it was a way of life.

He'd quietly assessed Khalid's every action for hours and was beginning to wonder where the man's loyalties truly lay. Could it be he'd placed his trust and Rachel's life in the hands of the enemy? He hoped not. Because if that were true, if he walked out of this thing alive, he'd probably be prosecuted for treason.

And he'd put Sam square in the middle of it as well. He'd completely ignored his commander. Hadn't returned any of his calls and hadn't bothered to keep him abreast of what he was doing. Director Hughes probably considered him the enemy by now. Michael was almost certain he'd dispatched someone to take care of him.

Possibly Rachel. Hopefully not Sam. All for what? Trying to salve his soul over Rahab's death. Because he was trying to make up for not listening to his best friend. As much as he hated considering it, all indications led to the conclusion that Booth had died working this last mission. Michael might not be skilled in field duty, but he knew Booth. If Booth were still alive, he'd have found a way to get word to someone by now.

Now, here he was, staking everything on the help of someone whose loyalty was murky at best.

"How much further?" he asked Khalid, mostly to kill the doubts swimming around in his head.

Khalid slowed his mount until Michael caught up. "Not far. About one hundred kilometers, give or take. Are you up to it?" Khalid's keen gaze speared him in the darkness.

Michael held his glance. He thought he saw the tribesman smile. "Yeah, I'm up to it."

"May I suggest we leave your man and my nephew to search the desert directly south and you and I head toward the village?"

Michael reined the horse to a halt. "Why would you suggest that?"

Khalid stopped his horse as well. "Look, my friend, I know you don't trust me, but I'm telling you I'm on your side. And I'm telling you, the less people showing up at one time, especially this hour, the less likely we are to draw attention to ourselves and the more likely we are to get the locals to cooperate."

Sam pulled up next to them. He'd heard most of their conversation. "It makes sense, Michael. The last thing we need to do is call the wrong attention to ourselves."

Michael considered it for a moment longer, mostly out of stubbornness. He knew what Khalid said was true and yet he couldn't quite dispel the feeling that Khalid was not being completely honest.

"All right. But you will check in every hour, Sam. And if anything looks off to you, no matter how small, you know what to do."

Sam nodded and then addressed Alain. "Ready?"

Alain gave Michael and his uncle a curt nod then kicked his mount into motion.

"Let's go," Michael barked to Khalid, who took the lead.

They'd covered less than five kilometers when Khalid's cell phone rang. He answered the call but kept his answers brief, further increasing Michael's suspicions of the man.

"Trouble?" Michael prompted when Khalid offered no explanation.

"No. My wife. She is concerned."

Michael accepted his explanation but didn't believe it for a minute. They continued their journey in silence. When they reached the midway mark, Khalid stopped at a small well.

"Why are we stopping?" Michael asked without bothering to hide his suspicion.

"We need to water the horses. A short break is in order."

Michael didn't believe him. He dismounted as well but made a point of keeping a hand on his weapon. Khalid drew water from the well using a bucket left there for that purpose. Michael led his horse to the water and turned away from Khalid. It was then that he heard it. The sound of a trigger pulled back into its firing position.

Chapter Nine

The lights of the village David instructed me to go to came into view. This was it. *Please, God, let David's contacts be reliable.*

With any luck, by this time tomorrow, I'd be home with my daughter. Then, I could leave the details of this nightmare for the pros to clean up. No matter how much I still loved Booth or how it destroyed me to think of what he must have gone through in those final moments of his life here on earth, especially if he'd sacrificed his life for mine, I'd had enough of these shadow games to last me a lifetime.

Driving in pitch darkness through unfamiliar territory, with fear my constant companion, it had taken me hours longer than I'd expected. By now, my appointed meeting time had come and gone. Would my contacts still be waiting for me? I didn't dare risk trying to reach out to David again.

As I reached the outskirts of the village, I slowed the Jeep's speed and took a moment to survey my surroundings. What I saw could barely be called a village. Little more than a row of shops and a scattering of small houses, there wasn't much to lend encouragement.

My arrival had to be drawing all kinds of attention, especially since I was traveling by Jeep and not normal means such as horse or camel, but I didn't dare risk leaving my only way of escape behind.

I held my breath and drove into the village. At first glance, there didn't appear to be anyone around. Not completely surprising considering the hour.

I spotted the heart of the town where I was supposed to meet the contacts. There was no one. I pulled the Jeep around to the side of what appeared to be some type of dry goods store. Some instinct I couldn't begin to explain told me to leave something personal in the Jeep. Something that could eventually be traced back to me.

I took out the picture ID with my fake name on it and left it face down on the seat then got out. I tucked the weapon I'd lifted from one of the men I'd killed into the pocket of my jacket, the cell phone I shoved into the other.

I kept in the shadows of the building as much as possible where there was a small amount of coverage. I waited in seclusion for what felt like hours before finally spotting them.

Two men, dressed in dark clothing, entered the village square. They stood next to what appeared to be some sort of gathering place. One of the men carried a paper. They were both nondescript. Average height and build, I could have been describing any of about a million different men.

I took a deep breath and made my way slowly toward them. The man holding the paper spotted me right away. He raised himself to full height and nudged his partner. They watched my approach cautiously.

"Laura?" The one with the paper, clearly the leader, asked. I detected a faint accent that sounded like a mixture of German and some type of Arabic dialect. It was so farfetched that I thought I had to be mistaken.

"Yes. Are you David's friends?"

The leader was the one to answer. "Yes."

I expelled a weary sigh of relief. "Thank You, God."

They smiled at each other and moved closer. "I'm sorry, there's not much time for introductions," the leader said. "My name is Hendrick and this is Mathoud. We need to leave. Now."

I slowly moved toward the Jeep. "I have transportation."

Hendrick shook his head. "No, there might be a chance someone has followed you. Please, we have a vehicle this way."

I hesitated, a tingling of uneasiness creeping along my spine. "Okay," I said at last, dismissing my fears. These men had been recommended by David. I could trust them. I followed them to the dark-colored SUV parked in the open.

Hendrick held the rear passenger door open for me. I hesitated only a second before climbing in. The vehicle had all the comforts of home, including leather seats and blessed AC.

I slumped back against the seat.

Almost home.

Mathoud peered back at me. "You look tired, Laura. We have a long journey. Perhaps you should rest." His accented voice held kindness. It wasn't reflected on his face.

"Yes, you're right. I am exhausted." I thought about what he'd said. "Where are we going from here?"

"To Sandifar, a small village near Kabul. There will be a private plane waiting for us where we will fly directly into Jerusalem."

I nodded, satisfied with his answer. I remembered the village of Sandifar. I'd seen it on the map. It was another one of those tiny villages prevalent here in this part of the world.

I thought about my daughter. I bet she'd grown a foot in the few days since I'd seen her last. I couldn't wait to hold her in my arms again and know this thing was truly over. With any luck, I'd be able to join Ava and David at the zoo...

I awoke with a start, uncertain where I was for a moment. What had awakened me? Some strange sound.

Then I remembered. I was safe. I was on my way home to Ava.

To my right, the sky blazed with varying shades of pink and orange. I'd been sleeping for hours. I rubbed sleep away and glanced around. Mathoud was now driving. He smiled at me. In the third row seat and directly behind me, Hendrick typed on his phone.

"Did you have a nice rest?" Mathoud asked.

Disoriented, I nodded. Something didn't feel right. I slipped my hand into my pocket. The gun was gone. As was my cell phone.

I glanced at Mathoud. He'd caught the movement. "You kept poking yourself and crying out. I thought it best to put your things out of your way. They are here in the seat beside me. Do you need your phone?" he asked pleasantly without giving anything away.

"Oh, no. No, I was curious."

Satisfied, Mathoud glanced back to the road ahead.

I pretended to be interested in the view outside of my window, but suddenly I was worried. Something Mathoud said didn't add up.

From what I'd learned about the small villages of the desert, most of them barely had any of the modern conveniences we enjoyed in the western world. Was it possible there would be an airstrip outside of a village as small as Sandifar? "How much further?"

Mathoud glanced my way again. "Not far. We'll be there within the hour."

I was beginning to doubt everything I knew. I didn't trust anyone. I wanted to be home. Wanted my life back to normal.

But David trusted these men. Why was I worried? After another hour of stark desert terrain, Sandifar came into view. I could see miles surrounding the village. I checked carefully, but I didn't see any airstrip, certainly no plane. I knew better than to ask questions at this point.

Mathoud maneuvered the SUV through the narrow streets to the opposite side of town where he pulled up in front of a small house.

I was conscious of Hendrick in the back seat behind me. He was gathering his gear.

"What are we doing here?"

"We are to wait here until our pilot arrives." Mathoud grinned back at me, dispelling some of the coldness from him. He got out of the SUV and waited.

With nothing else to do, I climbed out as well and followed Mathoud, aware of Hendrick bearing down close behind me. Whether or not this was intentional or not, I certainly felt trapped.

The house consisted of two sparsely furnished rooms. One served as a living and apparently a bedroom if the pallet in the corner was any indication. The other room was the kitchen. I assumed the bathroom would be outdoors.

I drew in a breath and forced my voice to remain level. "How long before the pilot arrives?"

"Soon, Laura. This will all be over with soon." Hendrick turned to me and smiled. Something in it told me my nightmare in Afghanistan was nowhere close to being over.

* * * *

Michael slowly turned to face Khalid. "What do you think you're doing?"

"I might ask you the same, my friend. Perhaps you'd be kind enough to tell me who you're working for." A sliver of a smile briefly lifted one corner of his mouth. "Why are you here?" Khalid held a small pistol against his temple.

Michael drew in a sharp breath. *No honor among spies...* How many times had Booth reiterated that point?

"I told you. I'm trying to find Laura."

Khalid shook his head. "Oh, I know what you tell me, but your actions speak differently. They make me wonder exactly whose best interest you truly have in mind. What purpose are you trying to serve here, my friend? Do you care if Laura lives? Because it almost appears as if you hope she doesn't come out of it at all."

"Put the weapon down, Khalid."

Khalid ignored the request. "Answer the question. You aren't here at your government's authority are you?"

"How could you possibly know--?"

"Because I've been watching you. You haven't once checked in with your superiors. You don't trust your own people. You're not acting under the authority of the U.S. government."

Michael stalled while considering how much to tell Khalid. How did a tribesman in the middle of the desert know about the CIA's inner workings unless he was more involved in matters than he led everyone to believe?

"How do you know CIA procedure?"

Khalid didn't answer. He nudged the pistol closer. "I would suggest you stop stalling and speak. Time is running out for more than Laura, my friend."

Michael's narrowed gaze swept over the man. He'd always trusted his instincts and his gut instinct was telling him Khalid was not the enemy. He blew out a breath and went for broke. "All right. I was sent here to bring Laura back. Alive," he added at Khalid's open skepticism. "I was given twenty-four hours to accomplish this or someone else took over and the outcome of the situation wouldn't be kind. That's when I found out she'd been kidnapped."

Khalid digested the information. "I see. Your people will want to put a lid on this thing before it gets out of hand."

"Yes. By now it's probably too late. I'm sure they will have sent agents here to take care of the situation."

"What do you mean, 'take care of the situation'?"

"What do you think I mean?"

Khalid understood. After a moment, he lowered the weapon. "Either they didn't have much confidence in your ability to diffuse the circumstances or they never intended Laura surviving hers."

Clearly, Khalid was no innocent when it came to the shadow games they played. Both scenarios were probably true. Michael chose to neither acknowledge nor deny the man's assumptions.

"What about you? What's your story? You weren't in the least surprised by any of this and if I'm not mistaken, I'd say you've done this type of thing before. I might ask you, *who* are you working for?"

Khalid appeared to waver.

"Who are you working for, Khalid?"

Khalid shook his head. "I work for no one. I am my own man. Now, I'm heading for that village. You can come or stay, it doesn't matter to me."

Khalid mounted the horse and moved away. With no

other option, Michael was forced to do the same.

They made the rest of the short journey in silence. Whatever secrets Khalid was keeping would have to wait. The most important thing was to find Rachel alive.

* * * *

"Forget the village. She's in Sandifar," Hughes barked into his ear.

He grabbed the map and flipped it open, searching for the new location. Sandifar was within a stone's throw of Kabul.

"Are you sure? How did she get there?"

"She's had help. And yes, I'm sure. Get there as soon as possible and get her out of there."

He tossed the map on the passenger seat once more and put the Jeep in gear. "I'm on my way there now."

He hoped this new twist in the plot wouldn't prove to be the worst of all. And the delay in reaching her wouldn't end up costing her life.

* * * *

"She's been here. Her ID's still here. She would have left it behind deliberately. She's giving us a clue. Something prevented her from returning to the Jeep. She left the area in a hurry." Michael's gaze held Khalid's. "I think we should search the area. See if anyone remembers seeing her."

"You think someone took her or she had to leave in a hurry?" Khalid asked with clear and present concern in every word. Michael suspected Khalid knew the answer already.

They both did. He feared canvassing the village would be a wasted effort, but it was an option and they were quickly running out of them.

"I'm not sure." This was obviously not the answer Khalid hoped for. With a dismal shake of his head, Khalid moved toward the first building, what appeared to be some sort of store and Michael followed. Laura's Jeep was parked close by.

The place was all but empty with the exception of a wizened old man leaning hard against a makeshift counter.

Michael faked ignorance to the language he'd excelled in during his CIA training while Khalid asked the patriarch if he'd seen the owner of the Jeep.

The old guy spared them a brief wag of his head before he shuffled off behind a curtained door separating the store from what was probably the owner's living quarters.

His answer wasn't any great surprise. Khalid questioned all four owners of the town's businesses in less than half an hour. Their answers were identical right down to avoiding eye contact and rushing off. No one saw a thing.

They were about ready to give up the search when an old woman sweeping out the front of a small eating establishment remembered seeing two men talking with a young woman late in the evening.

"Did you get a good look at her? Is this the woman?" Khalid asked in Arabic. He showed the woman Laura's picture ID.

She nodded. "Yes. That's her."

"And the men?"

"Foreigners. Like him." She pointed to Michael. "But they had a big black motor vehicle."

"Did you see what direction they were traveling?" She gestured in the opposite direction from which they'd entered the village. They were heading farther into enemy territory.

Khalid thanked the woman, and then he and Michael stepped outside into the heat of the early morning.

"Well?" Michael prompted, to keep his cover intact when Khalid remained silent.

"The old lady remembered her. She said she met with two men here last night. They left in a black vehicle, heading north. She recalled the men spoke English. They were not Arabs."

Michael shielded his eyes against the glaring sun. "Who are these men? Who could Laura possibly know in the place? She doesn't have any connections here."

"Perhaps someone from your team?"

Michael considered the possibility. The more likely option was not nearly as pleasant. Had Hughes taken things into his own hands? If that were the case, Rachel was trusting the wrong people to get her to safety.

And if that were true, then he would be found as guilty as Hughes. The time for secrets was over. "I hope not. Because if that's the case, then she's in more danger than she would be from the people who were holding her hostage."

They'd returned to the Jeep by this time and had

begun searching for any further clue Rachel might have left there. Khalid's sharp gaze locked on his. "What do you mean by that, my friend? I think you'd better explain yourself."

"I'm saying it might be in the best interest of *certain* people if she remains silent. And no, I'm not talking about me. I want to save her life."

"She knows something? Something that wouldn't set well if it were made known to the world?"

Michael threw protocol out the window. "Exactly. She knows too much. She's former CIA. She's seen things."

"If that's the case, then why were *you* sent here?"

"To bring her in--alive," he added when Khalid's arched one dark, menacing brow.

Michael saw all the questions, the speculation. His last chance at bringing Rachel home alive was quickly disintegrating around him.

"Look, is there somewhere that we can leave the mounts? I think we'd make better time in the Jeep, don't you?"

For a moment, he believed Khalid would refuse. After another tense second clicked by, the tribesman motioned toward the restaurant. "I trust the woman at the restaurant. I'll give her money to care for and feed the animals. I'll have Alain send someone back for them in a few days."

Michael took his answer for consent. "Good. Thank you."

Khalid didn't respond right away. He continued to watch Michael with those fathomless dark eyes. "Don't thank me. I'm not doing this for you." Khalid got out of the Jeep without another word. Michael followed after a minute's consideration of all the wrong he'd done in the past twenty-four hours.

With the animals secured, they returned to the Jeep.

Michael started for the driver's side then reconsidered. He didn't know this territory. His lack of knowledge could get them both killed. Khalid was knowledgeable in every aspect of surviving in the desert.

"You'd better drive." Michael climbed into the passenger seat and Khalid got behind the wheel but didn't budge.

"Not so fast. You need my help. I need answers."

Michael swallowed his frustration with difficulty. He owed Khalid the truth. But time was running out for Rachel. If what he suspected were true. The men she'd left with were not her friends. They'd been instructed to kill her. He and Khalid might be too late already.

"I'll explain everything on the way." Michael held up a hand when Khalid appeared skeptical. "I swear. I'll answer anything you want to know. We don't have a whole lot of time to debate the matter here. We need to be on our way."

The two men's gazes locked in a silent battle of wills. But Khalid at last recognized he was telling the truth and gave in.

Once they'd reached the outskirts of the village and Khalid was assured they hadn't been followed, he shot Michael a glance that meant it was time for Michael to start talking.

Michael grinned at the man's persistence. "All right.

I told you that the agent Laura came here to find was CIA. I take it she told you she was a former agent as well?" Khalid affirmed. "You know that Agent Tanner was sent here to try and capture Zyad Ali-Arawar. But what you don't know is Agent Tanner and Laura were sent to take out Bin Laden several years back before Bin Laden was actually killed. There were other agents already embedded within the Bin Laden organization as well as several informants working with them."

While Khalid watched the road ahead, Michael could tell he had his full attention. "Rahab was one of them?"

It was hard to think about the woman he'd once loved as dead. She'd always been vibrant. Alive. Willing to do anything to please him...and he'd walked away.

Khalid shot him another questioning glance that demanded a response before adding the obvious. "Evidently the mission didn't go well, otherwise, things would have turned out differently that day in September."

Michael agreed. "No, it didn't go well at all. In fact, it was disastrous. All of the agents assigned to the mission were captured. We couldn't go after them because technically they weren't supposed to be there in the first place. Their instructions were to contain the enemy, no matter what the cost. Two of the agents were slaughtered immediately. Tanner and Laura were taken prisoner."

"And the other agents involved?" Khalid spared him a glance.

"We never heard. They were never seen again."

Shock was identifiable in Khalid's expression. "I

see," he managed with difficulty, his opinion easy to read.

"If the extent of that mission's failure and this one were to become public knowledge, then someone would have to be held accountable."

"And you think by keeping it a secret you're doing what's right?"

"No. But I'm hoping the end justifies the means."

"And do you still have doubts who the bad guy truly is in this situation?"

"No. I think I know the answer." Michael had long ago stopped believing that because he had the backing of the U.S. government, the murky politics and shady bedfellows his team used to fulfill their missions were right.

"If Laura is a target and your government has abandoned Tanner and her both, what makes you think they won't come after you next?"

"There's a good chance they will. Which is all the more reason why I need to find Laura and get us to safety. If they can't get us, I'm betting they won't risk exposing past crimes to find us."

"How are you and Tanner connected? Are you his commanding officer?"

He couldn't explain it, but for some reason, Michael wanted to set the record straight. "Yes, in a way. I was his handler. I was the one responsible for sending him on this last mission. But Booth and I were more than coworkers. We went to university together. We were best friends for an awful long time. That's something I'd almost forgotten. I let the next mission, the job, the *cause* get in the way."

Michael's awareness of Khalid slipped away as memories of Booth dominated his thoughts. He'd gone over those last few days before Booth's disappearance in his head a million times. He'd let Booth down, both as a friend and as a commander. Booth was toast, he needed out. Michael ignored all the symptoms and probably let his friend walk right into the trap that had been set for him.

He turned away from Khalid's probing gaze. He hoped he was wrong. But if it were too late to get Booth out, then he'd do whatever he could to save Rachel. He owed that much to Booth.

Chapter Ten

"How much longer before the pilot arrives?" I asked Hendrick again. We'd been sitting in this small house for hours without any conversation or any contact from the outside world.

"Soon. Within the hour." His gaze slid to his partner who sat reading a German newspaper. "Why don't you try and eat something?"

"I'm not hungry. I want to get out of here. The longer we wait here, the more likely we'll be discovered. We should proceed on foot."

The corner of Hendrick's mouth lifted into a meaningless smile. "That would be foolish. You are safe here, Rachel. Don't worry."

Rachel! Rachel? How did this man know my true identity? I struggled to guard my reaction. As I studied his expression, nothing showed. Was he aware of the slip-up?

Mathoud stopped reading the paper and watched us both carefully. He'd caught it. I tried to appear normal. I turned away and started my pacing again. After another minute and a warning glance Hendrick's way, Mathoud returned to his paper.

The exhaustion that permeated from every pore of my body coupled with the pain of the wounds that had begun to itch like crazy made it next to impossible to think clearly. I'd started second-guessing everything and everyone. Had the two men always referred to me as Rachel? I struggled to recall. I was almost certain they'd called me Laura up until this point. Perhaps David had told them my real name.

Somehow, I couldn't believe that. David knew never to give away information that might compromise a cover.

"Someone's coming." Hendrick, who had been standing guard near the window, turned and headed for me. "Get out of sight," he barked.

Mathoud got to his feet and drew his weapon. I went to do the same but remembered my only means of defense had been taken away.

Mathoud motioned to Hendrick, who took my arm and pushed me into the tiny kitchen area. Mathoud waited until we were out of sight before stepping outside.

I could hear him talking to someone, followed by another man's voice. They were speaking in English. They kept their voices low, but I was able to make out Mathoud asking what took so long. The man indicated the entire area was hot. Meaning crawling with the enemy?

Mathoud stepped inside. "It's okay. It's him," he

announced, presumably for Hendrick's sake.

Hendrick released his death grip on me and I followed him into the living area.

Mathoud made a grand production of introducing me to the new player, in hopes of keeping me calm. "Laura, this is Bruce Johnson. He is the pilot who will be flying us out of here."

Johnson, a thin man with a receding hairline, wasn't quite what I'd pictured when I thought about a pilot working this area and flying such dangerous assignments. After a moment of awkward silence, he smiled at me. It was the type of smile meant to dispel all doubts. For me, it didn't quite work. "You look as if you've fought a war on your own. Are you ready to get out of here?"

I forced myself to answer. "Yes. More than ready."

"Good, then I think we'd better get moving." He turned back to Hendrick. "The place wasn't safe to land. I had to put her down some distance from here in the desert. We should get going."

Hendrick clearly didn't like being ordered around by the pilot. "All right. You will ride with us."

The trip out of the village seemed to take forever. And I was counting every second of them. With the end in sight, it felt as if everything was taking longer than expected.

Hendrick crept through the empty streets until we reached the outskirts of town. Then, open desert spilled out before us for miles. We topped a small sand dune, and there in the middle of the miles and miles of sand sat a helicopter instead of a plane.

The pilot jumped out and ran for the copter. Mathoud got out and opened my door. "We need to hurry. We were followed."

I climbed out and looked behind us. There was no other vehicle approaching. I'd kept a careful eye in the mirror for any sign of someone following us. There was nothing.

"I don't see anyone," I challenged.

Mathoud didn't like my answer. He took my arm and forced me to the copter. "They are coming. I've seen them. Hurry."

He almost picked me up and shoved me in the cabin, then jumped inside, still glancing nervously behind us.

Hendrick took his place next to the pilot. Within minutes, we were airborne.

As I squinted at the area below us, there was still nothing to indicate we'd been followed. The uneasiness in the pit of my stomach kicked up another notch or two.

Mathoud caught my glance. "Perhaps I was mistaken," he said with a careless lift of his shoulders.

He'd lied to gain my cooperation. "Where are we going?"

Mathoud hesitated for a long time before answering. Too long. "The pilot will take us to Germany."

I didn't believe him. I nodded, then pretended to look out the window as the mountains bordering Iran came into view.

* * * *

"They're airborne," Hughes announced without any

preliminary greeting.

He wasn't surprised by the news, but he was frustrated. "Do we know where they are heading?"

"Not yet, beyond the mountains of Iran. Get to Kabul. There's a helicopter waiting for you there."

"I'm on my way. What about the others? Any word?"

"No." After a moment, Hughes added, "If this thing turns bad, I may need you to clean up the situation."

He hoped it wouldn't come to that. To the man on the other end he said, "I understand. Once I'm airborne, I'll check in. In the meantime, call when you have anything. No matter how small."

He was less than a mile away from the village where she was believed to be held when the call came in. Kabul was north of the area. He turned the Jeep around and headed for Kabul, then called his man.

He didn't answer. Which could mean anything. Or the worst possible thing. He closed the phone and dropped it to the seat beside him.

The hours slid by every bit as unnerving as fingernails raking across a chalkboard. When the capital came into view, he chose to skirt around Kabul, to the private U.S. military base outside the city where the copter would be waiting for him.

He breezed through the tight, high-level security clearance of the occupied city with a simple flash of his credentials. His man was easy to pick out.

"You Smith?" the pilot asked. Not picking up on the fake name, he couldn't quite cover his tension. The man knew. This wouldn't be an easy assignment. It would be dangerous.

"That's right. Are we ready?"

"Waiting for you, sir."

"Good. Then let's get going. We're behind as it is."

When the copter was airborne, he asked the pilot, "Any word?"

"They are most likely going to Mashhad."

"Oh no." He'd expected this move but hadn't looked forward to it. "Can you get us in there?"

"Of course," the pilot assured him. "But you'll be on your own from there. I can't stay on the ground long. The place is too volatile."

He wasn't surprised. Afghanistan was bad, but the area they'd be flying into today was every man for himself. This was the place known as al-Qaeda's gateway.

Small factions of terror cells fought against others for dominance, tribes against tribes, leaving the area in turmoil and without safe harbor.

"How long before we land?"

"Another half hour."

"Good." He called Hughes.

As usual, Hughes got straight to the point. "They've landed somewhere near the border. I'm sorry I cannot get you more help. It was hard enough getting someone to fly into that area as it was."

"I understand. That's no problem. I'm used to operating alone."

"The pilot has the supplies you'll need to finish the job."

"Good. Anything else I should know?"

"Only that the chances of your phone working in that area are next to none. You'll be on your own most of the time. Be careful. You know what's at stake if you are caught."

"Yes. I understand."

"I'm counting on you to handle this. Don't let me down."

As usual, Hughes signed off without any further word, satisfied his command would be fulfilled.

He tried his informant one more time and the man picked up.

* * * *

"Ten minutes to arrival. You'll have maybe five minutes to get out of the copter before I have to take off again. Make it quick," the pilot announced.

Below them, the mountains disappeared and the rugged region of Iran's border replaced it. He found the supplies the pilot was instructed to bring along and shoved them into his backpack. By the time the pilot brought the copter down safely, he was armed and ready. The pilot hovered the craft some four feet above the ground. He jumped, tucking arms and legs into a fetal position. Rocks and hard earth greeted him as he rolled away from the helicopter. He found his legs and ran, keeping low to avoid the copter's blades. He'd spotted a group of buildings a short distance from the landing strip. He signaled to the pilot to take the copter up then sprinted to the first building that looked as if it had, at one time or another, taken heavy fire from the air.

With the copter out of sight, he secured the backpack tighter on his shoulders to take the brunt of its weight then took a minute to listen. The copter had barely cleared his line of vision when he heard it. The sound of vehicles, more than one, making their way to the area. Someone knew of his arrival. Whether enemy or friend, he didn't plan on sticking around long enough to find out.

* * * *

The insistent ringing of his phone distracted Khalid. He didn't see the weapon until Michael spoke. "I think you need to answer that, my friend. Apparently someone is worried."

Khalid glanced sideways and attempted to reach for his weapon. Michael obviously read his intent and said, "I wouldn't if I were you. I've grown fond of you. I'd hate to have to kill you, but make no mistake. If it comes to that and you try anything, I will in a heartbeat. Now, stop the Jeep."

With the gun inches from his temple, Khalid did as Michael asked. Khalid didn't doubt for a minute Michael would follow through with his threat. He brought the Jeep to a halt.

"Put the phone on speaker and answer the call. And I'd advise you not to give anything away," Michael ordered.

Khalid recognized the number and knew who would be on the other end.

"Yes," Khalid answered the call in less than a steady

voice. He glanced at Michael as the man on the other line began to speak.

"Keep Bernard distracted as long as you can. They've left the village and are heading for Mashhad, Iran. I need time."

Khalid cleared his throat. "Okay."

The mystery man didn't suspect a thing. The phone went silent on the other end. With nothing left to do, Khalid closed his and faced Michael.

"I'd say it's time for you to be honest with me, wouldn't you? Who was that?"

Khalid kept quiet, but Michael clearly guessed some of the truth. "CIA, correct? You've been working with me, having me believe I could trust you when the goal was to keep me out of the way. What's going on? Who are you working for?"

Khalid considered the question for an eternity, battle raging within him. "Yes, he's CIA. I know him only as Smith and nothing more. He was sent here when you didn't report in to your commander."

Michael digested the information then smirked at Khalid's clear lie. "Nice try, but he's not after me. He's after Laura. Why?"

Khalid breathed out a sigh. "I don't know."

Michael edged the barrel of the weapon closer. "Uh-uh."

"Shoot if you like, my friend, but it's true. I know little, in fact. Only that I am to keep an eye on you. Because you are considered to be a traitor."

"Hughes. I should have known he'd turn the tables on me. I'm no traitor." Michael shifted in his seat to face him. "Khalid, listen to me. The man you are working for is here to take out Laura. And me, no doubt. What's in it for you? What did they promise you?"

Khalid shook his head in disgust. "Apparently, nothing. I agreed to help your people because I thought I would be helping destroy al-Qaeda and the Taliban's stronghold. Keep ISIS out of our region. But it seems to me your team have their own agenda, which has little to do with helping my countrymen and I'm not at all sure who the real enemy here is. And to that I say do what you want. I've had enough."

Michael watched him for a second then lowered the weapon. "Me, too. I'm sick of this game. There will be no winners or losers here. Only more innocent victims. All I care about now is getting Laura out of here safely for her daughter's sake and for my friend's. I owe him that much. Beyond that, I don't care anymore." Michael shook his head in disgust. "Will you help me do that?"

Khalid studied Michael's expression for a long time and then accepted his answer. "I believe you mean that. Yes, I will help you. But you understand we are far behind the others. We'll need to get airborne soon to get there before it's too late to help."

Michael considered this. "I can get us in the air and to the area. Do you know the place where we're heading well enough not to get us killed?"

"I can try. The area is dangerous and I'm not talking strictly political danger. The conditions in that area are terrible. We will have no means of traveling except by foot. We should notify your partner and my people. Someone needs to know where we're going."

Chapter Eleven

The copter set down, not in Germany, but in enemy territory. I tried to keep from panicking when Mathoud ordered me outside.

"Why are we landing in Iran?" I challenged, hoping I didn't sound like the nervous wreck I was inside.

Apparently, Mathoud was still trying to garner my cooperation. "Laura, we don't have much time. This area is dangerous. If we're discovered, we will be shot on the spot."

"What happened to Germany?" I still hadn't budged.

Mathoud blew out an annoyed breath. "Our destination was discovered. Someone found out we were heading in that direction, which, of course, was exactly what we wanted. No one will be looking for us if we follow the border, but we are in Iran and it is extremely dangerous the more time we spend here. We need to get moving."

I stubbornly refused to move a muscle from the helicopter. Something told me that if I did, I'd be leaving behind my last chance of being found. Alive, anyway. "We're hiking out of here?"

"No. We have transportation." He motioned toward an approaching SUV. "Our guide to safety. First, you have to leave the helicopter. Now, please."

I was about to refuse again when the back passenger side window of the SUV lowered and David's face appeared.

He smiled and all my worries melted away. David beckoned me toward the vehicle. "Rachel, it's okay. You can trust these men. Please, you must hurry."

I jumped from the helicopter, ignoring the hand Mathoud extended to help me.

David opened the door. I rushed inside and into his open arms. I'd never felt safer.

When I actually let myself believe he was not a figment of my imagination, I asked, "David, what are you doing here?" I still held him tight, afraid he might disappear.

"I'll explain everything in a moment. First, we need to get out of here." He waited until Hendrick and Mathoud were inside before he instructed the driver to get started. Two men I didn't recognize were seated behind us.

A shiver of uneasiness slipped down my spine. "David, what's going on?"

"I'm sorry for all this cloak and dagger stuff, Rachel. Somehow or other, word got out to the wrong people that we were getting you out of there. I think that was my fault. They obviously had my phones monitored and I didn't realize it."

The explanation certainly made sense. Whoever was after me would have done their homework and discovered my identity soon enough if they hadn't known it from the beginning.

I shook my head, exhaustion numbing my usual analytical skills. "David, none of this adds up. Why would someone want to hurt me?"

"I don't know. I certainly don't understand any of it. My only concern right now is getting you to safety. We can sort through the rest later on when you're safe." He took a moment to look me over. "I'm sorry, my dear. You look like you have suffered a great deal."

Seeing David again reminded me of my daughter. "I'm okay. How's Ava?"

"She's well. Dana and Hannah have been indulging her. She misses you terribly."

For a moment, I couldn't speak. "I miss her, too."

David clucked his tongue at my tears and patted my hand. "This will all be over with soon, my dear. Only a little while longer. Perhaps you should rest. You look as if it's been a long time since you got a good night's rest."

I smiled at his thoughtfulness. "Yes. I feel as if I can sleep for a week."

"I cannot give you a week, but you do have a couple of hours. Use them wisely."

Still, I couldn't completely let go of my worries. "David, I think this is all related to the peace talks coming up next week. I'm certain someone is planning to do something."

He patted my hand again. "Let's not worry about that for now. You need to rest."

I leaned back against the headrest, content with his answer. My eyes stung from lack of sleep and physical exhaustion. My body ached. The places where the wounds had begun to heal itched like crazy. But I was safe. I was with David. And this crazy nightmare would all be over with soon.

The temperature inside the SUV was blissfully warm. The rocking motion the vehicle made as it climbed the rough terrain soothed me. Before long, I was asleep.

* * * *

I awakened to stillness. For a moment, I was disoriented. When I opened my eyes, there was nothing but darkness. I looked around. David was watching me. The SUV had stopped.

I glanced out the window and saw through the pitch darkness what resembled a house. I turned back to David. "Why are we stopping here?"

He nodded toward the house. "This house belongs to a friend of mine. We'll be safe here. Come. Let's get you inside and in a real bed."

My thoughts were still muddled from sleep. I didn't move. "But why are we stopping *here*? Shouldn't we keep moving to safer territory?"

He reached for my hand and squeezed it. "Rachel, I didn't want to alarm you, but we've gotten word that someone is tracking us. They'll expect us to show up in Algiers. It's safer this way. We can hide out here until the danger is gone. Come, Rachel, it's freezing in here."

I allowed him to help me from the SUV. "Watch your step. There's ice and slush everywhere."

I glanced up at the dark bulk of the place. Though the others had entered the house, the lights remained off.

"What is the first thing you and Ava plan to do when you get back home?" My attention was drawn back to David by that question. He was smiling at me.

"I don't know. I think I want to hold her for a long time. To reassure myself she's okay."

He chuckled and then stepped up onto the porch. "Yes, well, I can understand that. She is precious. I regret that I may have inadvertently fibbed to her in promising I'd take her to the zoo, but I wasn't expecting this new glitch."

This new glitch?

He opened the door. The house was still dark. Suddenly, I didn't want to go inside.

"Wait, David, how well do you know these men?"

He seemed offended by my question. "I trust them with my life." One strong hand was suddenly positioned against my back. He pushed me inside. The force of the action sent me flying across the floor with enough speed to crash into the opposite wall. The pain that seared along my back assured me I'd reopened several of the wounds there and probably added a few new bruises as well. I blinked back tears.

At first, I thought I'd imagined the whole incident until I got a good look at David's expression. The cold emptiness in him took my breath away. I knew this was no safe house.

And David was no friend.

Someone hauled me up from the floor with force. A stabbing pain shot down my neck and along my spine. But the physical pain was nothing compared to the emotional agony ripping apart my world, my heart.

I'd walked into the worst betrayal of all time. The man I thought was like a second father to me had now turned into my worst enemy.

No, please God, no.

My body grew weak. My legs could no longer support me. I was falling. Then I realized the pain I'd felt in my neck had been a needle. In a matter of seconds, the drug coursed through my body. My last coherent thought was that I'd willingly given my daughter over into the hands of my enemy.

* * * *

He circled back behind the rapidly approaching vehicles. There were three in all. They appeared to be some type of military. They'd been watching for the copter. Someone had tipped them off.

He'd expected them to comb the area, searching for him. Instead, the vehicles headed toward the mountainous area. Which meant, he wasn't their top priority.

On foot, it would take forever to follow. He'd need to find another means of tracking them. He searched the remaining building for some means of transportation but found nothing.

There was a small storage building at the end of the row. It was locked.

He took the butt of his gun and smashed it against the lock. It took several tries before the lock popped free. Inside, he found a less than encouraging Jeep, several cans of gas along with a wealth of explosives.

After the fifth fruitless try, he was almost ready to give up when the Jeep's tired engine cranked to life. He hauled several spare cans of gas and some explosives into the back of the Jeep then began following the caravan of vehicles. There was enough light from the moon and stars to make the road ahead somewhat visible. He didn't dare turn on the vehicle's lights.

He kept the Jeep at a speed that allowed him to keep the vehicles in view, but hopefully would prevent them from spotting him.

If what he suspected were true, the people in those vehicles were searching for Rachel. It that was the case, he needed help. He called Hughes and miraculously managed to get through.

"I'm in Iran. I'm following three vehicles. I think they're tracking Rachel. Get me help, now."

"I'll do my best. I'll have someone on the way. Do you trust your contact?"

He jerked the Jeep's wheel, barely missing a tree stump in the middle of what passed for a road. "Yes."

"Call him in. Get him there. He can reach you before my men can get there."

"All right, but hurry. I have a feeling Rachel's time is running out."

He stopped the Jeep and pulled out a map and small pen light from the backpack. He needed to calculate the best place to rendezvous with his contact.

Retrieving his cell phone from his pocket, he called the man. "I need your help. How soon before you can get airborne?"

"We'll be in the air in minutes."

He breathed a sigh of relief. "Good. I need you to meet me."

His contact said something he didn't catch and was forced to have it repeated. "All right, we'll be there within the hour."

We'll be there? There was no room to spare, certainly not time to question. "Good. You'll be arriving around the same time as me. I'll see you there."

* * * *

Michael turned to Khalid and asked what could only be described as a pointless question. "Are you ready for this?"

Khalid did little more than nod.

"Right. Here goes nothing." Michael wiped the sweat from his brow as they approached the military base. With any luck, Hughes hadn't put out warnings at all the bases yet. Otherwise, he'd be arrested the second he set foot at the base outside of Kabul.

Security was unusually tight. Something was definitely in the works. The guard at the entrance spotted his and Khalid's approach. Michael brought his fake ID, which was pretty much standard procedure for most agents traveling in enemy territory.

He'd had the bare essentials for creating an alternate ID for Khalid as well.

While Khalid drove, Michael took his picture ID and superimposed it to his alternate ID.

He handed it to the tribesman. "It sucks, but I'm hoping the men at the base won't check it too closely. It's all about the attitude you approach them with. Let me do the talking. And take off the robe, will ya? At least give us a fighting chance. I'll drive."

The two guards lowered the security arm at their approach.

Michael could sense Khalid's uneasiness growing. "Relax. I'll handle it."

Michael had his ID out and waiting and instructed Khalid to do the same.

"May I help you, Agent Blake? Agent...Stephens?" He glanced briefly at both their IDs then sized them up, his gaze remaining on Khalid, who obviously didn't look like a Stephens.

"Yes, I have orders to meet Commander Hughes in Algiers. I need transportation there immediately."

The soldier clearly was suspicious. "I've received no word from any Commander Hughes concerning this. I'll need to call it in."

"Fine, if you want Hughes breathing down your neck, and probably having your job as well as mine, go ahead."

The soldier eyed him carefully. At least he'd caused a moment of doubt. "I beg your pardon?"

"Commander Hughes has given me specific

instructions to meet him there in one hour. If I am delayed, it could be a matter of national security. Now do you understand? Do you want that on your hands?"

"Sir, I have orders to verify all incoming and outgoing flights. I'm just doing my job."

"And I'm telling you this is your job, soldier."

After a glance to his partner, who seemed frozen in place at the turn of events, the young and clearly inexperienced and overstressed soldier shrugged. "Okay, but if this comes back to me, it's on your head, Agent Blake. I'm not taking the rap for this."

He opened the guard post and let them pass through. When they were a safe distance from the soldier's hearing, Khalid released a deep breath. "That's all fine and good but how do we get airborne? Can you fly?"

Michael turned to him and grinned. "As it happens, I can."

Chapter Twelve

I awoke to ice-cold water thrown into my face. A bright light, so blinding that I couldn't see anything beyond it, was trained directly on me. Once again, my hands were bound above my head. My body was weak from the drug they'd used to sedate me.

It seemed to take forever to get my bearings through the drug-induced fog. Then I remembered David's betrayal.

"Ah, good, you're awake," David acknowledged in that same jovial tone he'd used a thousand times in the past to update me on the latest happenings at work or perhaps spread a little office gossip.

The depth of his betrayal to both me and our country, and possibly Booth, was immeasurable. It took forever to voice my condemnation. "David, how could you do this? How could you betray me, our country, and the people we're entrusted to protect? For what?" It was hard to form coherent thoughts anymore. Torture and sleep deprivation had that effect on the human body. Not to mention the fact I hadn't eaten anything substantial in days.

He appeared taken aback by my shock. "Why do you think? You left me with no other choice when you insisted upon going after Tanner." David moved close enough for me to see the rage and yes, the hatred, in his eyes. "You couldn't leave well enough alone, could you? You had to insist upon searching for him and see where it got you. You know too much, Rachel. I'm sorry, but you have to be taken care of."

I shook my head to clear away the cobwebs. "Know too much? I don't know anything about what you're talking about."

"Oh, come now, Rachel. Do you honestly expect me to believe he wouldn't have told you anything about this?"

"Who? Who are you talking about?"

"Stop playing games. You know who I'm talking about. Booth Tanner. Your lover."

My mind struggled to keep up with his accusations. "Booth? I haven't seen Booth Tanner in years and you know that. What could he have possibly known about you? What are you involved in, David?"

As I watched, the man I considered a father figure changed in an instant. Gone was the caring man with which I trusted my child's life. In his place was a cold, calculating stranger.

He motioned to someone behind him. When the man stepped into the light, I recognized him in an instant. It was Hussein. He stalked close enough for me to smell his foul breath. The leer on his face confirmed the truth.

The punishment I'd endured at his hands the last time would seem like a cakewalk compared to this round.

He grabbed a handful of my hair and twisted it tight. Several clumps pulled loose. I couldn't hold back the cry of pain.

Unmoved by my suffering, David addressed me again. "You have a choice, Rachel. I can make sure your death is painless, or I can guarantee you suffer dearly. It's up to you. Tell me what you know about the weapons."

I kept my gaze fixed on David. I wanted my torment embedded in his memory. "What weapons?" I asked through gritted teeth. "I told you, I don't know what you're talking about."

David blew out a put-upon sigh then motioned to Hussein once more.

The man released me, then held something up for me to see. It was a stun gun. With one quick movement, he lowered his hand and aimed the device against my right side. Electrical current shot from the weapon, the pain excruciating as the voltage fired through my body. My heart rate kicked into a frightening tempo.

After what felt like an eternity, Hussein removed the gun. My legs turned to jelly. I slumped against my restraints, losing consciousness for a second or two.

More water was tossed in my face. I took my time trying to steady my pulse before my heart exploded in my body. Slowly, I opened my eyes.

Hussein stood close, waiting for the command from David.

"Rachel, please tell me what I want to know. Do you

think I enjoy seeing you hurt this way? It breaks my heart. You were like a child to me."

"Don't give me that!" I spate the words out. My gaze locked once more with his. David shook his head and then signaled Hussein into action. He made a show of raising the voltage up another notch. He jabbed the gun against my side and the pain seared through my body like a wildfire out of control. My body jerked and convulsed as my heart pounded out of control and a welcoming darkness overtook me.

When I awoke again, I was lying on the floor, my hands and feet bound. Although the room was dark, someone close by smoked unfiltered cigarettes. I could hear voices. I recognized David's right away and Anwar's as well. Anwar asked David to let him kill me and be done with it. I was wasting their time.

"Don't be foolish. She might know something she's told the others. We cannot risk it."

"Then let me have a turn at her. Hussein is weak. I can get her to talk."

Hussein was quick to voice his opinion. "You speak foolishness. What do you know about interrogating prisoners? I worked for Saddam. I know how to break a prisoner."

Anwar gave a derisive snort.

As I continued to pretend unconsciousness, David put an end to it. "You are both wrong. She's a former agent. She's too good for you. There's only one way to get her to tell us what she knows. Anwar, I need the child."

They were going after Ava as leverage against me. A

helpless terror any parent would feel when they were unable to protect their child washed over me. I tried to think beyond it. I couldn't let them hurt my baby. I'd do whatever they wanted, make up a plausible lie if it meant saving her from pain.

Anwar came over to where I lay and nudged me with his foot. "She's awake."

David followed, along with Hussein. "Are you ready to talk yet?"

I sat up slowly, buying time.

"Don't be a hero, Rachel. I wouldn't want anything...distasteful...to happen to Ava. You know I love her as if she was my own and it would kill Hannah if the child was harmed, but I will do what I have to do. I cannot go to prison. Not even for Ava. I'll ask you one more time, what do you know about the weapons? Who have you told?"

I drew in a shaky breath and prayed my hunch was correct. "All right. You want to know who I told. Everyone. All of my former colleagues at the CIA. They're on their way as we speak. They'll be here at any time."

The expression on his face would have been comical under any other circumstances. "If that were the case, then you wouldn't have come here in the first place. You're lying, Rachel. Do you think I don't know you well enough to tell when you're lying to me?"

"You think? Are you willing to bet your life on it? Are they?" For a second, he hesitated. I held my breath. This was my last shot.

Then he turned to Anwar. "Get the girl. Maybe

watching her daughter suffer for a while will jog her memory."

It took everything in me not to take the bait. David and his entourage of henchmen left me alone. There was only one choice left. I had to find a way out of here. I could get word to Dana before Anwar could make good on David's threat.

* * * *

The house appeared large and rambling. Dark. The men searching for him had gone inside less than a half hour earlier. He'd counted twelve. Who knew how any others were inside? Or what they'd done to Rachel.

He'd broken radio silence long enough to give his coordinates to Hughes.

"You have until 0400 hours to get her out of there. Do you understand?"

He glanced at his watch. Less than an hour. Next to impossible with an army of troops watching his back. "Yes, I understand. I'll take care of it."

"Get in touch with your man and have him set down near Moumar."

He disconnected the call. He was one step ahead of Hughes. He'd contacted his informant already and given him the location for the meet. He hoped his man was the only one listening in. Otherwise, the people in the house would kill him before he could think about saving Rachel.

He used the night vision goggles but didn't see any type of outside security. Slowly, he left his vantage spot to examine the house for a point of entry. Other than the front entrance, there were plenty of windows, all of which were locked. He made his way around the house. There was a back door situated at what appeared to be the kitchen area.

Someone had left a light on, which made it risky, but he couldn't wait any longer. He jimmied the lock until it released then crept inside and stood stock still, listening for any sound within the house.

Bits of conversation drifted down the hallway to where he stood. He cracked the door to the kitchen and followed the sound. The voices came from an open door. He eased to a position where he could see into the room, hopefully without being spotted.

From his vantage point, he counted seven men, all dressed in dark military type apparel. Where were the others? He slipped past the door.

The place was certainly large enough to possess a basement. He imagined they'd be holding her there. It would offer the right amount of security. They'd know she was former CIA.

He found the stairs after two tries and a dozen adrenalin rushes. He crept his way down, one careful step at a time until he reached the bottom.

There were three doors at the bottom of the landing area. He tried the first two but came up empty. The last was locked.

The lock proved a little more of a challenge than the last. It took him several hair-raising minutes before the lock sprung free. The room was dark. He stepped inside and let his eyes adjust to the darkness. After a second or two, he spotted what appeared to be a lump in the corner. Then, it moved.

* * * *

I was no longer alone. Someone opened the door and stepped into the room. Whoever it was didn't turn on any lights. This couldn't be good. I'd been working on the knots on my hands since David and the others left.

I froze when the person came near. I could smell the masculine scent of soap and male reaching out to me. After a second, he knelt in front of me.

"Rachel, thank goodness. I was afraid I'd find you dead." I'd expected a fate worse than death. Nothing prepared me for seeing my under director, Jeff Scott, staring back at me in relief. *Jeff?*

"Jeff? Jeff, what are you doing here?"

He began hurriedly untying my restraints. "There's no time for explanations now. There's a dozen or more armed men up there and I don't think they're up to any good. I need to get you out of here."

"Jeff, David's here. *He's* the one responsible for this. It was David all along. Do you think he killed Booth?"

Jeff paused for a second to look me in the eye. "I don't know. Let's get you out of here and to safety and then we can figure the rest of it out. Can you walk?"

His non-committal answer made me believe Jeff knew more than he was willing to tell me under these circumstances. It all but confirmed Booth's death. I forced myself to answer him. "Yes." Tears slid silently down my cheeks, giving much away.

Jeff reached beneath his jacket to where he had a second weapon holstered. "Here, take this." He helped me to my feet, but I refused to lean on him. I'd finish this thing the way Booth would have. They way he'd taught me to finish a mission.

"I'm fine. Lead the way."

He gave me a quick assessment, then seemed to decide I was telling the truth. Jeff made his way back to the door and I followed close behind. He stopped to listen for a second then cracked it and looked out.

"Okay, let's get out of here. We don't have much time."

I grabbed his sleeve and whispered desperately, "Jeff, David is going after Ava. He's trying to use her to gain information from me."

He stopped long enough to look at me. "That won't happen. We have Ava and Dana. They're both safe. We figured David might try to use Ava against you."

My legs almost gave out on me. I blew out a sigh of relief. We'd reached the landing when he whispered, "Stay behind me. If we make it out alive, head for the woods to the north of the house. There's a Jeep waiting there. If I don't follow, keep moving north to Moumar. There's help on the way there."

Jeff cautiously opened the door. The place seemed silent enough, which in itself was frightening. As we made our way down the hall, one of the doors opened. Jeff pushed me inside another room. It was a bathroom.

"He's probably coming this way," he whispered. He searched the small closet-like room. There was a shower with a curtain. "Get behind the curtain." Jeff lifted me into the space then made sure the curtain was in place before flattening himself behind the door.

The man swung the door open and stepped inside then closed it again, not bothering to turn on any lights. Jeff grabbed him before he knew what hit him. He snapped his neck, then eased the man's body to the floor.

"Help me get him into the shower. If anyone comes looking, I don't want them to find him right away."

We struggled to maneuver the man's dead weight into the shower. With the curtain covering him from view, Jeff peeked out the door to make sure no one else was coming. Slowly we headed through the house. It seemed to take forever, and I realized I'd been holding my breath. With freedom close, I didn't dare hope.

We'd reached the kitchen when I heard it. The sound of helicopters, more than one, flying in at a rapid speed.

"We've got to get out of here. They have the coordinates. Their orders are to capture the men alive as they flee the house, then destroy all evidence of the place. I don't think they'll take the time to ask our names. Hurry, Rachel." Jeff dragged me through the door and outside. Shouts came from inside the massive structure as we cleared the yard.

Then Jeff lifted me into his arms and ran. We'd made it to the edge of the woods when the spotlights from the first copter hit the house.

Jeff didn't stop until we were outside the group of trees and into a small clearing where the Jeep was parked. Jeff dumped me into the passenger seat and climbed into the driver's side. He started the Jeep, put it in gear, and floored the vehicle.

The Jeep barely had time to lurch into motion when the horizon behind us was engulfed in gunfire. Shock and awe.

"Oh my..." I couldn't take my gaze off the sight. It looked like Armageddon had broken out behind us.

Jeff's cell phone shrilled to life. "Yes. We're fine. She's banged up, but I'd say otherwise okay." Jeff glanced my way. "Yes, I'll see you there."

We'd covered another couple of miles in silence as I waited for answers. When none was forthcoming, I finally turned in my seat to face him.

"What happened back there?"

Jeff barely spared me a glance before he focused on the bumpy, rutted dirt road in front of him. "I'd say a couple of bad people got what they deserved, wouldn't you?"

"And what about you? Whose side are you on?"

He quirked that familiar grin my way. "Yours, of course."

"Then who are you working for? Obviously, it's not the State Department."

Jeff laughed at that. "No, but I was kinda enjoying playing the brown-nosing nerdy geek for a while." He glanced at me again. "You have to admit, I was pretty good at it."

He was right. I thought about all the times I'd resented Jeff for what I thought to be his wanting my job. I never suspected him of being a spy. "Yes, you were good at it. Who do you work for, Jeff? I think I've earned the right to know, don't you?"

He agreed. "Yes, fair enough. I'm CIA. I've been working undercover for Director Hughes since I started with the State Department. We've been investigating a security breach within the department."

This piece of news had my full attention. "A security leak? What type of security leak?"

"No, not a leak, I said breech. Someone within the department was using their power to communicate with terrorist cells operating in the Middle East. They were being paid a lot of money to move weapons of mass destruction through the area undetected."

"WOMD? David was transporting WOMDs to terrorists? But, he's Jewish."

"Yes," Jeff said quietly. "But I guess they were willing to overlook that fact to get what they wanted."

I couldn't believe what I was hearing. "When did you find out about the breach?"

"A little more than two years ago. We'd been trying to find the connection for a while without any luck. Then we raided a known terrorist hideout and found information that led us to believe the person we were looking for was one of our own. It seemed virtually inconceivable. I was sent in to investigate. I started with the usual. I checked everyone's background, including yours." He confirmed my unasked question.

"Booth? How does he fit into this?"

"Booth got a lead from one of his contacts."

"Rahab?"

Jeff shot me a strange look. "Yes. Through her help, we captured a fairly high-ranking member of al-Qaeda and soon discovered the name of our man inside. David.

We needed to prove it. I'd say we have now."

"I don't get it. He's been like a father to me. I've known him for a while. David has no vices. It's inconceivable. Why would he do it?"

"Everybody's got their dirty little secret, Rachel. I dug deeper into his financial records and found out David was in debt up to his head. Overextended on all his credit cards. Apparently, David has a gambling problem. I guess it's true what they say, money is the root of all evil."

"But I thought Booth was sent to take out Zyad Ali-Arawar?"

Jeff shook his head. "That was his cover story. We didn't know who we could trust including our own people."

It was impossible to take it all in. My thoughts reeled. I'd been so caught up in trying to understand David's act of treason I hadn't realized Jeff had brought the Jeep to a stop in what appeared to be a small airfield.

"What are we doing?"

"We're getting out of here. I don't doubt that our guys took care of the situation back there. But we are in enemy territory and I don't want to take the chance of someone witnessing what happened and coming after us."

Within minutes of our arrival, another Blackhawk helicopter appeared over the treetops. Once the copter touched down, Jeff got out of the Jeep and came round to my side.

"Ready? We need to hurry, Rachel."

I opened the door and got out, but Jeff refused to let

me walk. He carried me to the helicopter. As I neared the copter, Khalid reached out his hand and helped me inside.

Once I boarded, I saw the pilot of the copter. Michael Bernard.

Jeff boarded next and shook Khalid's hand. "Glad to see you two could make it. Glad you proved not to be a traitor, Agent Bernard."

"I appreciate the vote of confidence," Michael said as he acknowledged both Jeff and me. I glanced at Jeff. He was as surprised as I was to see Michael. It was easy to read the animosity between them.

Khalid spoke and broke the tension. "We were beginning to wonder if we'd be too late. Now, if no one has any objections, I'd like to get out of here before our luck runs out."

"You were the one Hughes sent to clean up. I should have known," Michael said with a touch of anger in his tone. He was not easily shaken, but clearly, he hadn't expected this twist. He spoke to Khalid while putting the copter in flight. "This is who you work for?"

"Sorry we had to keep you in the dark, Bernard, but Hughes wasn't willing to take any chances when the stakes were this high." Jeff tried to smooth the waters, but Michael didn't go for it. His pride had been wounded by being kept out of the loop.

I waited until we were airborne and heading for safety before turning to Jeff. As much as I dreaded the truth, I needed to know answers. "I think it's about time you told me what really happened to Booth. Don't you?"

Chapter Thirteen

Jeff had known the minute she had time to digest everything she'd want answers. Still, he wasn't prepared to tell her the truth yet.

He didn't miss the warning glance Bernard threw him. Since the beginning, he'd worked close to Rachel and gotten to know her pretty well. She was a woman of integrity and courage though at times she seemed to doubt those strengths in herself. He'd quickly dismissed her from the list of possible traitors. From past intel they'd received, he knew whoever was responsible for aiding in the weapons transfer had to have a high-security clearance.

Discovering it was David had been like a blow. Everyone who knew the man thought he was as good as they came. A true peacemaker.

It would be next to impossible to sweep this mess under the rug. Especially now, with the world's attention focused on the Middle East and the upcoming peace talks.

David's absence from them would take center stage. "Jeff?"

He turned to her. She waited expectantly. "I don't know, Rachel. We're not sure if Booth is alive or not. There's been a report."

Fear clouded her expression. "What type of a report?"

"A body of a male has turned up near Kandahar. In the desert. A white male fitting Booth's description."

Her hand flew to cover her trembling lips. "How soon before you know for sure?"

He glanced Bernard's way again. "Not long. We have people on the way there now."

She shook her head, buying his answer for the moment. "And David?"

"We're still waiting for the final analysis." Michael evaded the question.

"Is he *dead,* Michael?"

"Oh, no. No, he'll pay for his sins dearly." Everyone in the copter knew what that meant. Rachel seemed to grow weary of the conversation for the moment. She'd need immediate medical attention once they arrived in Kuwait.

The remainder of the trip was made in tense silence. Jeff reflected on the future. There would be many changes to come. The events of the past would demand it. He hadn't wanted to tell Rachel the truth about David. How he'd be interrogated and forced to give over names then turned over to the Israelis where he'd be dealt the final justice for his crimes. But, considering her past, he had a feeling she'd know.

* * * *

When I awoke again, I was lying in a hospital bed. I didn't remember a single thing beyond those first few moments of the flight. I glanced around the room and saw Jeff keeping watch while working on his laptop.

"Where am I?"

He smiled when he saw I was awake. "Royal Hospital in Kuwait. I thought it best to make sure you were okay before sending you home."

"Ava--"

"Is fine. She's waiting at home for you. Want to get out of here?"

I knew there were many things that he wasn't telling me but for the moment, my concern for my daughter far outweighed my curiosity.

Once I was dressed, Jeff told me there was a private plane waiting to take us back to Jerusalem.

"Are you returning to Jerusalem as well?"

We sat in the back of a limo while the driver inched his way through heavy airport traffic. "Yes. But don't worry. I'm not after your job anymore. My instructions are to make sure you get home safely to your daughter."

"What about David's position at the peace talks? This will be devastating."

He nodded solemnly. "The talks will be postponed another week. The world will be told David is retiring due to bad health."

"Impossible. If someone from the press doesn't get wind of the truth, there's no way we can get whoever steps in to David's position updated by then."

"Oh, I don't think you'll have a problem getting up to speed, Madam Ambassador."

I sat up straight. "What are you talking about?"

Jeff, in his usual manner, simply grinned and shook his head at my ignorance. "Congratulations. You've been appointed to fill the position, Rachel. The word came through this morning. You were David's original choice anyway, which was the one thing he did right. You're ready. Do good things with it. Make up for David's mistakes. Leave a positive impact in the Middle East."

I looked away from the tenderness in him. "Yes. I'll try." My thoughts were all over the board. There would be much to do. Many challenges, first and foremost, the upcoming peace talks. Did I want to take over that nightmare? In the past, it had always seemed some future event. Not anymore.

With the plane airborne, I thought about all the questions I needed answering.

"What happens to Hughes? He may have pulled this one off in the end, but he's as guilty as David in many ways."

Jeff hesitated for only a second. "He's been asked to resign. Again, it will be done quietly so as to not raise suspicion."

"And Michael?"

"I'd say that will be up to the new director, wouldn't you?"

I took a deep breath and asked the question I'd been arguing with my heart over for a long time. "Jeff, tell me the truth. Is Booth dead? Please, I need to know."

The length of time it took him to respond had me believing I had my answer already. "That depends."

I shook my head, sick to death of playing games. I needed the truth, not more confusing words. "Enough, Jeff. Tell me the truth for once. I don't understand. How could Booth being dead depend on anything? What does it depend on?"

He looked me square in the eye. I'd never seen Jeff more serious. "On you. Booth's death depends on you, Rachel. On whether or not you want him to be dead."

I searched his expression, trying to understand the hidden meaning. Then it hit me. Booth was alive. Jeff knew this for a fact. Booth hadn't wanted to tell me.

It hurt like crazy to consider Booth would have chosen this course. But, did I want him to be alive? I had a decision to make. I'd made so many mistakes in the past thinking I was doing what was right for Ava. This time, I needed to be sure. I owed it to Booth and to our daughter.

I took a deep breath and accepted the truth. I'd never stopped loving Booth no matter how far I'd run or how hard I'd tried to deny it. "I want him to be alive. I need him to be alive," I said with all my heart. "I have to know if he...still cares. And I need to apologize for not telling him about Ava."

Jeff nodded then turned away. Not exactly, the most reassuring of answers but all that I would get for the moment. I'd take the small amount of hope he'd given me and be happy. Booth was alive. No matter what our future might be together, we'd always have Ava to share. My daughter needed her father every bit as much as I needed her. I had no right keeping him from her. And I'd spend the rest of my life trying to make it up to both of them.

Chapter Fourteen

Two weeks after the peace talks ended with only a slim margin of success, Booth Tanner found me. Seeing him again after such a long time cleared away the last of my doubts. I still loved him. I'd been a fool to walk away from what we had.

I'd spent the morning with Ava playing in our backyard. I think she'd somehow known how close to dying I'd come although I'd tried to keep it from her. She didn't want to let me out of her sight for a minute and I was okay with that.

Since my imprisonment, I'd been an emotional wreck. In the past, I'd never been a weepy person. Coming close to death had changed that. I'd wake up in the middle of the night my heart racing. In my dreams, I was right back in the prison, facing the man I'd once believed to be a true patriot. David had destroyed so many lives and he'd taken away my ability to trust. I was determined to get it back. I wasn't going to let him win.

When Dana offered to take Ava to the zoo, my daughter was just excited enough to be away from me for a couple of hours. As hard as it was to let her out of my sight, I needed to find a way to make peace with what happened and put it in my past.

The doorbell rang a few hours before I expected them home. Had Dana forgotten her key? I opened the door and saw him standing before me and for a second my knees threatened to desert me. I couldn't believe it. Booth was alive and here and I didn't know what to say to him.

"Hello, Rachel." In the most unexpected place, Booth stood before me like a promise from the past waiting to be fulfilled.

The sound of my name coming from him took me back to the past. I loved everything about Booth. The way he always looked fantastic after we'd spent the entire night tracking a bad guy. The hazel in his eyes. The tousled dirty blond hair, so like Ava's, touching the collar of his cowboy-style shirt. Further proof that Booth was a rebel who cared little for current trends. He'd told me once he'd lost track of the number of times he'd been reprimanded for the length of his hair. He'd been ordered to cut it many times, but he'd refused. The shirt, well, that was typical Booth, a cowboy at heart.

Seeing him here, in my element and unexpectedly, well, my mind went to places best left for later. If there was to be a later for us. If he'd still have me. Right now, he looked as if he'd stepped out of bed and was ready to take on any bad guy. And that was the mystery that was Booth Tanner.

"Rachel?" I loved the way he said my name. When I met his gaze at last, my next breath simply evaporated into the tense space between us. He sounded hesitant, unlike Booth. Today, there was a hard edge to him I hadn't seen before. It scared me. It spoke of the things Booth had endured since we parted. It tore at my heart. Would he ever be able to put those horrors behind him?

"Booth, I-I..." I struggled to find something to say while my thoughts scattered into a dozen different directions. "It's good to see you again."

He stepped inside and closed the door. A sad smile played at the corners of his mouth, not dispelling the hardness in his eyes. "Is it? I would have thought otherwise."

Suddenly, a thousand different memories flew through my head. All the times we'd laughed and fought. Loved each other. I wondered if this would be the final chapter for us. Two strangers tied together because of one little girl and one troubled past.

The thought brought tears. Before I could hide them, he'd seen. Booth stepped close, a breath away from me.

I saw the truth in him before he even said a word. "No, Rachel. It will never be like that for us."

Before I could consider the consequences of my actions, I went into his arms as if I belonged there. Booth was both safe and dangerous, as he had been in the past. As I wanted him to be now.

I wrapped my arms around his waist and held him for a moment longer. I felt Booth wince, then I pulled away to look at him. "Are you okay?" While he rushed to reassure me he was, I knew he had been through hell and back. As hard as it was to voice the words aloud, I needed to hear his answer. "What are we doing here, Booth? I can't be with you. I can't risk losing you again."

Another tiny smile, this one genuine, lit up his face. "I'm not going anywhere. Well, except maybe back to D.C. long enough to learn the details of my new position within the agency. I've been offered Hughes' job."

I think it took me longer to believe I'd heard him correctly than it did to believe he was alive. He laughed at my expression. That tenderness I'd always loved was there. The same as the night when we'd made love in the desert. "It's true. I accepted with only one stipulation. My home base will be here in Jerusalem. With you--with our daughter."

There were many things I wanted to tell him and much I needed to ask his forgiveness for, but that would come in time. It could wait. Right now, I wanted to tell Booth how much I still loved him. But the words wouldn't come. Not that it mattered. He knew. I could see it in the way he smiled at me before he took me in his arms, kissed me and showed me he felt the same.

"I love you, Rachel," he told me with so much sincerity that I believed him.

"You really mean that?" I asked in amazement. I sounded so uncertain and so vulnerable.

"Yes. Yes, I do. I love you. And I know that you love me. I was wrong before. I thought I wasn't capable of loving anyone until I met you. But you changed that for me. I think I fell in love with you the first time we met. You remember?" He smiled down at me.

I did. I remembered the cocky, self-confident man he'd been back then. "I think I fell in love with you too and I don't want to live without you in my life a moment longer. I love you and I want to try--" With a desperate sound, he pulled me into his arms, his lips claiming mine once more, capturing the rest of my words with his kiss. I couldn't believe he was here, holding me, kissing me. I was so afraid I'd wake up and find myself alone again.

* * * *

"Want to take a walk?" he asked some time later when I was finally able to let him go.

It was time to settle the issues between us once and for all. Talking was the hard part. In the past, I'd always dreaded this discussion. But not now, because I knew no matter what, we loved each other and we'd work the rest of it out, in spite of how difficult and painful it might be.

"Yes. Ava should be back in another half hour so we should have time." I grabbed my cell phone, and Booth's hand.

Close to my house, there was a small park I'd grown to love. I came here often when troubled. Today, I felt the same, only different. I found my favorite bench and sat with Booth close by.

"How long have you known about Ava?" I asked when I couldn't stand the doubts any longer.

"Since the beginning."

"Michael?"

He shifted next to me. I could feel the heat of desire in his eyes. "Yes. In spite of what you think, Michael cares about you, Rachel. He wanted to do what was best for you and Ava. But he wanted to be my friend as well."

"I'm sorry." I barely got the words out before the tears came. Booth gathered me into the shelter of his arms and held me.

"Rachel, don't. Please don't cry. You did what you thought was right for our daughter. I could never hold that against you. And you were right. Back then, I wouldn't have made a good father, but I have to confess, not being part of her life almost killed me."

I never considered Booth might actually want to share Ava's life. I'd been so determined I knew what his reaction would have been that I never let myself trust him. "I'm sorry I did that to you."

He squeezed me closer and shook his head. "No, you did what was right."

"What changed your mind?" I had to know.

He let me go, but only to look into my eyes. "Rachel, I always wanted to be part of her life…and yours. You have no idea how hard it was to honor your wishes. But I'm glad you changed *your* mind. Was it because of what happened in Afghanistan? With David?"

I wasn't sure where to begin to explain my change of heart. "Partly, but mostly it was Rahab's message--and my reaction to it."

At last, it became clear. Booth wasn't surprised to

hear she'd contacted me. He'd told her to. "You told her to get in touch with me."

"Yes," he said and watched me carefully.

"Where were you, Booth? I was so afraid for you. Why did you want me involved?"

There was so much pain there that I wanted only to comfort him. I cupped his face with my hand. "It's okay. We don't have to talk about it."

"No, I need you to know everything." His fingers reached for my hand and brought it to his lips. "I never wanted you involved in this thing. Especially when David was identified as the mastermind. I wanted to keep you as far away from it as possible, but I had no choice. You see, I was injured. I couldn't get word to you on my own. And I didn't know who to trust but you."

I searched his expression. "Injured. How bad is it? Please tell me--"

He squeezed my hand. "I'm okay. But at the time, I wasn't. I was in the small village in Afghanistan that you went to search for Rahab when I discovered the truth about the WOMD and the impending attack on the talks. Or at least part of the truth. At the time, we still had no idea about David. Unfortunately, David's goons were there as well. There was an attack. I was shot. One bullet missed my heart by inches." He stopped. Breathed. Brushed aside my tears.

"Rahab took me in, got me to safety. Got medical help. It was then that it was decided the best way to draw out the person behind this within the embassy was to let them believe I was dead. We had no idea it would play out this way. I had no idea you would come after me, I thought you'd go to David for help and that would help flush out the person behind this thing."

I smiled a little at this. "Did you think I'd leave you there alone? I couldn't do that, Booth. In spite of what I tried to tell myself, I still loved you...and we are still married." I quickly confessed the truth about not being able to sign the divorce papers.

He smiled in wonderment. "I'm certainly glad you didn't."

"How did Rahab become involved in this? I know you don't like to use civilians."

"She's not--wasn't--a civilian. Rahab was the sister of Zyad Ali-Arawar. She saw the terrible things her brother and Bin Laden were responsible for and she was worried about her people and her country. She came to us to help."

"I'm sorry that she became a pawn in this thing." After a moment of silence, I asked about David. "What will happen to him?"

"He'll be turned over to the people he tried to harm. They'll deal with him. For now, he's singing like a canary. He's provided valuable information that will help us take down dozens of terrorist cells, maybe bring in Zyad Ali-Arawar."

When did this become so widespread? If we took down all of al-Qaeda, I knew it wouldn't end there.

Booth read my thoughts. "I wish I knew the answer, Rachel. How many more good people have to die because the human race can't coexist? None of us are innocent in this. The U.S, Afghanistan, al-Qaeda. ISIS.

Me, David, Rahab. We all have blood on our hands. And it won't end in our lifetime or Ava's. We can only do our part and hope."

"Booth, I know at times the lines seem grayed, but you are on the right side."

He smiled, but the hard look had returned. "Yes, I hope so. But why doesn't it feel that way?"

Because I had no answer for him, I changed the subject. "What happens now for Michael? He must be disappointed. Hughes had to be grooming him for the position."

Booth's grin reminded me of a kid in a candy shop. "Are you kidding? Michael can't wait to get back into the field. He missed it. He'll be in charge of the hunt for Ali-Arawar."

"Is that wise? Michael's field experience has to be a bit rusty. It's been years."

"He'll catch up quickly and he has some good men backing him up. Sam...And Jeff. I think Michael wants to try and make up for the mistakes he made in the past by trusting Hughes. For sending me out on an assignment he knew I wasn't in the right frame of mind to finish." Booth caught my surprise and shook his head, adding gravely,

"Yes, he was my handler, but don't hate him too much for that, Rachel. Michael has his own demons to contend with. He still blames himself for leaving Rahab. I believe he truly loved her at one time. With Sam and Jeff's help, he can make a difference in the war on terror. It won't bring back Rahab or the past, but it's a start for seeking redemption."

I hadn't spoken to Jeff since I'd left the hospital, but I wasn't surprised he'd chosen to return to active duty.

It could be addicting once you got a taste of it. "And you? How are you going to adjust to being behind a desk most of the time?"

He took his time answering. Booth's fingers stroked my face, brushing back a strand of my hair. "When you left me, well, nothing was the same. I felt as if I'd lost my center, my passion for the job. To tell you the truth, I've wanted out for a long time. I didn't think I had anything to go home to. I hope that's changed. I hope I have you and Ava."

Years had passed since I'd walked away from Booth and the shadowy games we played in the name of freedom. During that time, I did everything to push him out of my head and my heart, but I hadn't been able to. I loved him. I realized I'd been waiting all this time for him to find me again. For the first time since that night long ago, I was hopeful.

I took a deep breath and looked into his eyes. I could probably have not said a word and he would have understood, but I wanted him to know how I felt, no, I needed him to know. After all, none of us knew how long we had on this earth. My final mission in Afghanistan proved that.

"Booth, I love you. I never stopped loving you. And I want to be with you. I want us to be the family we were meant to be and I'll do whatever it takes to prove that to you. If it means leaving my position with the embassy and returning to the States, then so be it. You and Ava are the only things that matter--" Whatever else I might have said died away the second his lips met mine once more.

When Booth Tanner kissed me, there was nothing else on my mind but him. The passion and intensity in his eyes right before his lips met mine made it seem as if we'd never parted. The gentleness in his touch, as he held me close, was all the forgiveness I needed.

Together we'd tell our daughter about her father and I'd make sure she knew what a hero he truly was. Together we'd put the bad things in our past behind us. We'd finish the shadow games we'd once been engaged in for the last time.

The End

Other Books by Mary Alford

Montana Skies
The Prodigal's Redemption

www.ingramcontent.com/pod-product-compliance
Lightning Source LLC
Chambersburg PA
CBHW050843180626
46814CB00007B/2593